The Marinolli Treasure

A Malenglish Novel

Written by Hal Lewis

Hal Lewis' The Marinolli Treasure

Copyright © 2007

ISBN: 978-1-4303-1192-8

www.Malenglish.com

Printed in the United States of America

July 2007

AUTHOR'S NOTE:

In this work of fiction all of the characters and events portrayed are either products of the author's imagination or are used fictitiously.

The historical information pertaining to past sale prices of the T-206 Honus Wagner card and the dates of sale, however, is factual information, as is the information about the companies who ordered and printed the card in 1909.

The only mystery still unexplained to collectors and historians today is how any of these cards exist when none were supposed to be produced or distributed due to Wagner not giving his permission. This book offers an informative and interesting solution!

As usual, some liberties have been taken in describing actual places and procedures to facilitate the telling of the tale.

Chapter 1

New York City
September, 1909

Frank Bowerman.

The Frank Bowerman!

Joey Marinolli could hardly believe his good fortune, as luck was not a common fruit to find growing on the Marinolli family tree in recent years. His immigrant parents had both passed away just two summers earlier from typhoid fever, so at age fifteen and without any other relatives, Joey found himself now living at the New York Foundling Orphanage and working odd jobs to help support himself and the mission. The pleasant memories of an ordinary childhood had all been suddenly whisked away from Joey like the scraps of cardboard that he had been sweeping into a pile just moments ago.

Being the assistant nighttime janitor at the American Lithograph Company was one of three jobs that Joey worked every day, and even though it paid him slightly less than the other two, it had recently become his favorite of the three for one simple reason: baseball cards.

Joey loved baseball more than anything because it was the one memory of his father that he could still cling to vividly in his mind. Before getting sick, Vito Marinolli had been a steel worker by trade, and his claim to fame around the neighborhood was that he had helped build the Polo Grounds where the famed New York Giants played their baseball games.

Vito had become a Giants fan through that connection, and he passed that allegiance down to Joey during countless hours of playing stickball in the street and reading together about the Giants in the New York Times. And at no time in Joey's life was the bond with his father tighter than it was during the summer of 1905, when the Giants were tearing up the National League.

While every other living person in their borough was idolizing New York's famed pitcher Christy Mathewson that summer, the Marinolli family worshipped at a different altar. Their favorite Giant was a big league journeyman by the name of Frank Bowerman, who just so happened to be a tenant in the same apartment building where the Marinollis lived.

Bowerman was such a bit player that none of the other occupants in the brownstone had any idea what the big guy in Apartment 3-C did for a living and why he traveled so often. But Vito and Joey knew, so they visited him in the evening after every home game to get a personal account of that afternoon's contest. Bowerman was more than happy to recount the day's events -- often sharing colorful anecdotes about opposing players -- and in return, the Marinollis were perfectly content with helping him keep his occupation under wraps around the building.

Led by Mathewson and their feisty manager, John McGraw, the 1905 Giants dominated their opponents all season long, winning the National League pennant by a large margin and then capping the year off with a rout of Connie Mack's Philadelphia Athletics in a new thing called the "World Series." Bowerman had been relegated to the bench by the end of the season due to his aging knees, but that did nothing to diminish him as a true hero in young Joey Marinolli's eyes.

In November of that year after the postseason games had ended, Frank Bowerman packed up his belongings and moved back to his native Michigan, but not before giving his game-worn World Series cap to a wide-eyed Joey as he waved goodbye from the front stoop. Needless to say, that cap was Joey's biggest treasure, and he kept it locked tightly in his personal trunk at the orphanage. His greatest treasure, that is, until now.

For the past several weeks, the American Lithograph Company had been working furiously on a new job -- printing baseball cards for the American Tobacco Company to insert as a brand new promotional item in their cigarette packages. And every night, Joey was charged with sweeping up the scraps of leftover cardboard and burning them in the incinerator. Occasionally he would catch a glimpse of a snippet of a Mathewson or McGraw card that had been miscut and left on the floor as trash, but he had yet to spot a card of Frank Bowerman.

Joey wasn't even sure if a Frank Bowerman card existed, since he had never been a big time player with great name recognition. In fact, Joey learned from older kids at the orphanage that Bowerman had just retired from baseball altogether in July when the team he had been managing, the Boston Doves, were mired firmly in last place of the National League.

The Doves were in deep financial trouble and rumored to be up for sale to James Gaffney, who wanted to rename them the Braves after his own nickname, the "Brave of Tammany Hall." In a cost cutting measure, the Doves had tried to save expenses by using Bowerman as both a player and manager in 1909, but the experiment had failed miserably.

This left Joey wondering if his hero would ever surface again in professional baseball. At age forty, Bowerman was well past his playing prime, and leading his team to a record of 22 wins and 54 losses in his brief managerial stint did not bode well for his chances of ever being hired to coach in the future.

So every night, Joey scrounged through the rubbish on the factory floor, searching for any shred of evidence that a Frank Bowerman card was being produced. He had no qualms about burning the bits and pieces of players like Ty Cobb and Walter Johnson every night, since they were nothing more to him than fictional characters that he would never meet. Joey knew, however, that his loyalty to his employer would be tested if a portion of a Frank Bowerman card should ever find its way into his pile.

In a way he hoped that he was never put into this dilemma, because Louis Ettlinger, the owner of the American Lithograph Company, had given strict orders against anyone "pocketing" any of the cards for personal use. Joey had seen Mr. Ettlinger fire other employees on the spot for what seemed to be trivial transgressions, so he stayed as far away as possible from the finished cards in order to avoid even a hint of suspicion. As much as he wanted the cards for himself, he valued his job even more.

There was normally a very tight watch on the actual cards themselves, which were stored in large boxes and kept locked in a huge storage room when Mr. Ettlinger was not on the premises. On a normal evening, when Joey would arrive at six o'clock to start his cleaning chores, the freshly minted sheets of cards were nowhere to be seen, having already been locked in the storage room or loaded and shipped out on that day's caravan of horse-drawn wagons. And since Joey was too young to buy cigarettes himself, he had no way of ever acquiring any of the cards for his own use.

But tonight was different. When Joey had arrived for work, Mr. Ettlinger was still in the factory, and was obviously peeved about something. Joey had heard him barking orders to Sal, Joey's direct supervisor, yelling something about "burning the whole damn lot." It was then that Joey noticed a stack of boxes eight feet high and five feet wide shoved over by the door to the incinerator.

As Joey began sweeping a heap of paper fragments toward the furnace, Sal came around the corner, wiping his brow with his sleeve.

"I don't care if it takes all night, kid, but you need to burn that whole batch of cards right there," Sal said, pointing to the boxes. "Apparently there's some big stink about one of the players on there, so the boss man says they all gotta go. Just burn the whole darned pile, boxes and all."

Putting down his broom, Joey nodded his affirmation of understanding and watched as Sal went back to his normal routine of scrubbing down the huge stone printing press in the other room. Joey strolled over and inspected the stack of cardboard boxes, each one about the size of a small suitcase with *Piedmont Cigarettes – Factory 25 – Richmond, Virginia* stamped across the top.

His first thought was that he was thankful he could fit the entire boxes one at a time into the opening of the incinerator without having to empty them and break them down. This would make his job a lot quicker and hopefully allow him to get back to the orphanage in time to get a big bowl of soup before they ran out for the night.

After a half-hour of laboring at the open furnace, Joey was drenched with sweat but had whittled the stack down substantially and was nearing the end of his task. If he could finish this up and rush through his sweeping chores a little faster than usual, he could still get that hot meal he was craving. Otherwise, he would be sleeping on an empty stomach for the third time that week.

Rejuvenated by the thought of food, Joey tried to hurry the task and grabbed the next box by the top flaps only instead of cradling it from underneath. The weight of the case forced the top flaps to come unsealed, causing Joey to lose his grip on the box as it slipped through his perspiring hands and fell flat on the floor with a loud thump.

Although the other two flaps on the top of the cardboard case remained sealed shut, there was a gap of about two inches between those closed flaps that allowed Joey to see a sliver of what was inside the box. Staring back at Joey from between the narrow opening were six sets of eyes, all belonging to a face that Joey would never forget if he lived to be a hundred years old.

It was an artist's rendering of Frank Bowerman from the torso up, shown beaming proudly in his white Boston Doves jersey against a light green background. And not just *one* image of Frank Bowerman, but at least *six* that Joey could see through the breach and apparently a whole box full of them!

From the size of the box and the six small Bowerman images that he could see vertically aligned through the gap between the closed flaps, Joey could tell that the uncut cardboard sheets in the box contained a total of thirty cards each -- five across and six high. Given the thickness of the individual cardboard sheets and the weight of the boxes, Joey guessed that each box contained roughly 100 sheets of cards.

Math was never one of Joey's strong suits, but he knew that he could multiply any number by a hundred by simply adding two zeros to the end of that number. Thus, it didn't take Joey long to determine that he was looking at three thousand Frank Bowerman cards just sitting there on the floor in front of him!

Waves of different emotions instantly began crashing through Joey's head. He was demoralized at learning that he had already burned about sixty thousand of his hero's cards, furious at Mr. Ettlinger for ordering their destruction and confused about why Bowerman's retirement from baseball had merited such a harsh action.

Did Frank Bowerman deserve to have his legacy wiped away forever just because he was a terrible manager? Or was Mr. Ettlinger just getting revenge at Bowerman for leaving the hometown Giants and playing for a rival? Either way, how could they do this to his idol?

Joey knew in a second what he was compelled to do, but stealing was the type of offense that would get him fired from his job and thrown out of the orphanage. At age sixteen, which Joey would be in three weeks, the orphanage was allowed to set him out on the streets as an emancipated minor if he didn't follow their code of conduct. While Joey looked forward to the day when he could afford to live on his own without the strict rules of the Roman Catholic facility, he knew that he wasn't yet ready to make that break.

But he had to do something!

He couldn't just stand there and set fire to the greatest personal treasure he had ever encountered, could he?

Checking over his shoulder to ensure that Sal was still in the other room, Joey bent down and closed the top flaps, pushing them firmly shut so that the adhesive agent would re-secure. Then without another thought, he hoisted the box up under his arm and bolted out the door!

He knew that Sal would hear the door open and shut, but Joey prayed that Sal would think it was just Joey going out for his usual breath of fresh air. The fumes from the print shop could get extremely nauseating at times, so it wasn't unusual for someone to step out into the street for a minute or two to steady himself.

Joey was sprinting down the sidewalk, furiously trying to reach the corner before Sal or anyone from the plant could step outside and shout an alarm about missing inventory. He had already formulated an excuse in his head for why he had run off from the job, and Joey knew that if he could get to the orphanage without being captured, he could lock up the box in his trunk and dash back to the factory in a matter of minutes. Sal might not even realize that he had been gone.

The worn leather soles of Joey's shoes slipped and slid on the bricks as he scrambled around the corner at breakneck speed, still tensing for the screams or whistles that he knew would come.

Finally after running for two more blocks and then darting through an alleyway shortcut, Joey stopped to rest and knew that he was safe! His heart was racing a thousand beats a minute, both with the adrenaline of the sprint and the thrill of the heist.

Joey knew that within a matter of minutes, he would have a hundred full sheets of Frank Bowerman baseball cards locked up inside the chest in his room. While he hadn't stopped yet to really ponder the trade value of these cards on the street, he was more exhilarated by the fact that he had single-handedly prevented the destruction of the only Frank Bowerman collectibles that would ever exist.

He owed that much to his friend, and Joey knew that his father would have been proud of his devotion had he been here to witness it. Joey knew that he would have to hurry back to the print shop and finish burning the rest of the boxes, but now he could do it with a clear conscience.

As he exited the far end of the alleyway and climbed the stairs to the orphanage, Joey was appropriately whistling a brand new ditty that was a smash hit all over Manhattan.

"Take Me Out to the Ball Game" – Albert Von Tilzer, 1909.

It was the first time since the death of his parents that Joey had any reason to be joyful at all, and he hoped that maybe this stroke of fortune was a sign that his luck had changed for the better. As he headed to his room, Joey had no idea that what he held in his hands would one day be so valuable that men would kill for it.

Chapter 2

Atlanta
2007

"*Shop Around*" – Smokey Robinson, 1960.

I wasn't even born at the time it came out, but I'd heard Captain & Tennille do their version of it in the early seventies and the point of the song was the same to an impressionable young boy: that I had better play the field until someone dragged me off of it kicking and screaming. After all, this was somebody's *momma* giving the advice in the tune, not some pimp or scumbag. I filed the recommendation away in my head and moved forward with childhood, knowing that I was still years away from even starting to play the game of love.

But as I entered the teenage years, my hormones were telling me it was time to start putting that sage motherly guidance to good use. Every girl was different and better looking than the last, so it all seemed so fresh and exciting. My fantasy for Mr. Roarke would have been a trip on the Love Boat with Charlie's Angels, but the list for that one was a mile long. Instead, I settled for hanging out at the local skating rink trying to score.

At pinball and air hockey, that is. I just couldn't fall in love: I couldn't shake those words of warning from years before out of my head. The fear of getting trapped in a relationship was stifling, so the best way to avoid it was to hang with the guys and pretend to be too cool for the girls. Hey, if it worked for the Fonz, it might work for me, right?

But one night I was getting ready to skate back on the floor after the couple skating session had just ended, and I heard it again. Just like Ray Kinsella heard the voice telling him to build it and they would come, I heard my own inner voice, and it came in the form of a new smash song playing over the loudspeakers:

"I Need a Lover That Won't Drive Me Crazy" – John Cougar, 1979.

I realize now, in hindsight, that telling someone to hit the highway wouldn't be the fatherly Mike Brady type of advice to give a young boy, but I didn't realize it then. All I knew was that if a famous rocker like John Cougar couldn't handle being in love, then a skinny kid like me wanted to avoid it like the plague. So what I took from the song was that Cougar had given me convenient, albeit selfish exit strategy for ending every relationship -- and I *had* to end them all as quickly as possible if momma wanted me to shop around, right? Again, I processed the data and stored it away in my mental library.

I know this might all sound crass and chauvinistic now, but you have to remember that I was just a young impressionable boy trying to captain a vessel on the sea of love with absolutely no experience or training. After all, it wasn't my fault we weren't learning about love and emotional connections in school. Instead, they were trying to teach us about the *science* behind the birds and bees. *They* were the ones telling me what to put where, and *they* were the ones instructing me to use condoms every time I had sex.

"Thank you, Jesus!" I remember thinking to myself. You mean I get to have sex even when I'm *not* trying to make a baby? *Now* it all made sense to me why these guys taking the buffet line approach to love had the right idea. Gentlemen, start your engines!

And if this all-you-can-eat smorgasbord concept hadn't completely taken hold inside of me yet, it was firmly cemented into my subconscious a year later when I entered high school. The girls had all grown into women, and they were proud to prove it. But they'd also become wiser, so they were now looking for true love -- not just a couple skating partner for the night.

My instincts told me that I should probably start exploring the concept of a long term loving relationship, when out of nowhere another hit record put a permanent end to any chance I ever had of becoming a one-girl kind of guy:

"Love Stinks"- J. Geils Band, 1980.

That one summed it up pretty clear and concise; no beating around the bush there. Those three songs formed the Holy Trinity by which I've lived my life, so is it any wonder that I'm forty years old now, have never been married, and still can't speak a single word from any of the three romance languages: French, Italian and Female?

I'm fairly attractive, reasonably athletic, and a junior law partner in one of the most esteemed sports and entertainment law firms in the country. In fact, I got my name on the firm's letterhead faster than any attorney in the firm's twenty-seven year history: I was eight when the firm of Evans, Steinberg & Conroy was formed.

Okay, *so what* if the "Evans" on the shingle is really for Charles Evans *senior*, my old man who graduated first in his class from an Ivy League college of law, and not for me, Chuck, who barely scraped through law school at the University of Florida? You think any of the girls that I'm trying to impress realize this distinction when I first introduce myself and tell them where I work?

Heck, no. It's like I've got a golden key that unlocks the door to the vault where a great treasure is stored! But my problem has never been getting the vault door open; it's been that I never learned the secret code words that apparently must be voiced before the treasure room of love can be safely accessed. I tried using John Cougar's words once, but had a slap mark on my face for a week afterwards. And it never even occurred to me what I had done wrong. I just assumed she wasn't a big fan of his after he added the Mellencamp.

So here I am, some thirty years after hearing *Shop Around* for the first time, and I've still never been unable to crack the mysterious code of romance. And not for lack of trying, mind you -- I try harder than freakin' Avis -- but at the end of the night, I ultimately end up sitting with my single friends and talking about the same old things.

Actually, we talk about all sorts of different things, but they would probably all still fall under one general classification of speech: Malenglish (Male English).

The *Merriam-Webster* definition of the word trivia is "unimportant matters," but how can anything be "unimportant" when it fuels the lifeblood of survival for one gender of an entire species? How can something be defined as "unimportant" when without it, 49% of the world's population would be functionally illiterate? The average male that I knew would probably be unaffected had the telephone never been invented, but take away his trivia and he would return to his infant form with no means of communicating to the outside world.

The dictionary is just flat wrong on this one, because the real definition of the word trivia is "anything that a female thinks is stupid."

Unfortunately, since I'd grown up with three brothers, no sisters and a matronly mother who made June Cleaver look like a biker chick, I didn't learn this until it was way too late. I was raised speaking only Malenglish around the house -- where the most important form of speech *is* trivia – and never had a relationship with a female long enough to ever realize that she wasn't understanding or appreciating a thing that I was saying. Thus, even to this day, watching me try to talk to a woman is something akin to viewing the filmed footage of the Hindenburg's final adventure. It always starts out fine, but by the end, the crash and burn sequence is just too painful to watch.

Thankfully for me and my primitive male friends, the beauty of speaking Malenglish is that any man can do it, regardless of his "emotional quotient" or whatever buzzword Dr. Phil is using these days to brainwash the female population and drive them into a frenzy of prejudice against those of us in the Malenglish-speaking world. What attracts men and offends women is that there are no *feelings* in Malenglish; they simply do not exist. They're like vowels in Russian or pig latin words that don't end in "ay"…there just aren't any.

If you don't believe me, I'll give you my best recollection of the two hours of conversation that took place between me and two guys from work at the bar the other night after the women had all judged us unworthy of invading their airspace.

> Me: *"Hold The Line."*
> Alex: "Asia?"
> Me: "No, they're *Heat of the Moment.*"
> Jim: "Survivor?"
> Me: "Nope."
> Alex: "Give us a clue."
> Me: "Okay. Kansas."
> Jim: "Kansas? Like the band? Like *Dust in the Wind* Kansas?"
> Me: "Nope."
> Alex: "Like the state? What is it, the 'Show Me' state?"
> Me: "Yeah, like the state."
> Alex: "Okay, hold on, gimme a sec, I'll get it. Kansas is the 'Show Me" state, so I'm gonna go with the word 'show' and see where it gets me. Who sang that song about his friends and a show that never ends?"
> Me: "That's *She's a Beauty* by The Tubes, but that's not the clue I was giving. And by the way, dipwad, Missouri is the 'Show Me' state, not Kansas."
> Jim: "Dude, The Tubes! That's a blast from the past! You know what else they sang?"

Me: "No clue; do you even know?"
Jim: "Yep."
Alex: "What?"
Jim: "*Talk to Ya Later.*"
Alex: "Oh, sweet! That's a toughie; I've got to remember that one!"

This was the closest thing to an "emotional connection" that ever occurs in the Malenglish-speaking world. Alex had paid the highest compliment possible to Jim by acknowledging Jim's trivia mastery and admitting that he will plagiarize it somewhere down the road. An important bit of male bonding had just occurred there that was nothing short of one girl telling another that she is the prettiest girl in the whole bar. Women would have seen this as two geeks talking about inconsequential crap; men would have recognized it as a rite of passage to the next level of the constant quiz show that is manhood.

Alex: "Okay, so *Hold The Line* is not The Tubes?"
Me: "Nope."
Jim: "Aw crap, I give up."
Alex: "Me too. Who the hell was it?"
Me: "Toto."
Alex: "Damn, I knew that. I *knew* that! What was up with the crappy 'Kansas' clue though?"
Me: "Toto -- like the dog in the movie, dumbass. You know, Kansas, Dorothy, tornado, munchkins, the freakin' lollipop guild."
Jim: You sure that wasn't *Willie Wonka* with the scary little people and lollipops?
Me: "No, it was definitely *The Wizard of Oz.*"
Alex: "Chuck, that clue sucked, man."

Me: "Well, I guess I could have slipped into my falsetto voice and started singing, "*Ro-san-na…Ro-san-na*," but I didn't think you needed a lifeline *that* easy, you doofus."

Alex: "Still, you could have given me something better to work with."

Jim: "Oh yeah, like what? Let's hear you come up with a better clue for Toto."

Alex: "Hey, did you know that in 1977, the three rookies of the year in all three of the major sports had the same initials? Got any guesses?"

Jim: "Wow, that's weird! Hold on, gimme a sec, I'll get it."

Alex had blown off responding to our challenge without batting an eye and had completely changed the subject. This is an extremely important part of the Malenglish dialect, as it helps us clumsy males stumble into our next conversation. Otherwise, we would be content to sit all night racking our brains to the answer for whatever trivia question was asked last. But I dare anyone to try using this "blow off and spin" move with a female after she's asked whether or not you like her hideous new outfit. You'll be back at the lonely guys table *real* fast.

Me: "Okay, 1977, right? I know the rookie of the year in football was Tony Dorsett because he won the Heisman in 1976, so we need someone in baseball and someone in basketball with the initials T.D."

Jim: "The only one I can think of is Tim Duncan, but he's twenty years too late."

Me: "How about Daryl Dawkins. His nickname was 'Chocolate Thunder,' is that it – Thunder Dawkins?"

Alex: "Uhhh…no. Do you think I would ask a stupid bush league trick question like that? Come on, man, this is serious."

As you've probably noted, speakers of Malenglish can hurl insults back and forth with reckless abandon. In fact, it is required, or the young cub will show his weakness and be eaten alive by the older males. I'm not sure what would happen if one girl told another girl that she was stupid and needed to shut up in front of a group of their female friends, but I'm guessing a phrase that rhymes with "loyal witch" would pop up about fifty times on the gossip wires over the following hours. To women, this would be legitimate grounds for a cat fight; for men, it's just two cats clawing around having fun.

Jim: "I can't think of anyone in baseball from the seventies with the initials T.D. This is a good one, but are you sure you got it right?"
Alex: "Yep."
Jim: "Screw it, I'm drawing a blank."
Me: "Me too. All right, you win. I've got no clue. Who were they?"
Alex: "Adrian Dantley, Andre Dawson…and *Anthony* Dorsett!"
Jim: "Aw man, that's bullshit! I *knew* it was Tony Dorsett! That *was* a bush league trick question."
Alex: "No, that's his full legal name. Nothing bootleg about that one."
Me: "Yep, he got us. That was a good one. The man's on fire."
Alex: "Oh golly, I'm hot today!"
Jim: "The Kid…*dun, dun*…is hot tonight."

Me: "And the only prescription, is more cowbell!"

This was a typical display of one of the most basic and fundamental tenets of the Malenglish language. Never, ever, ever say something in your own words if you can get the same thought across using a famous quote from a movie or *Saturday Night Live*. In this short span, we saw a *Caddyshack* reference followed immediately by some Loverboy lyrics and then a classic from *SNL* as the cherry on top.

To some females, this rapid verbal onslaught may seem as difficult to perform as a triple toe loop after sticking a triple Salchow, but to men it comes as natural as channel surfing or ignoring a ringing telephone. We don't know why we can do it and women can't -- it's just in our blood from birth.

There.

That was all of it.

It took you probably five minutes to read it, but it took us about two hours to act it all out last night. Granted, that's probably because we spent a great deal of time looking at all the scenery in the bar while we mulled over our trivia, but a picture's worth a thousand words, right?

Then why is it that every time I go see a motion *picture* with a date, she wants to go home and spew ten thousand words about the *picture* show we both just saw? Wasn't the whole point of going to see the damned movie together so that we could share the experience and *skip* the whole talking thing? But pardon me, I digress.

The fact of the matter is that I'm just a Malenglish-speaking guy who never developed a sense of romance or relationship, just like I never developed a tail or a third ear. I blame my DNA…and the Captain & Tennille, of course.

Ah, but don't start feeling sorry for me just yet, because there is a huge bright side to all of this!

My ability to speak and translate Malenglish at a doctoral level has made me a huge success as a sports agent for all of our law firm's male clientele. My dad may be the rainmaker who brings in all the business, but I'm the guy who's responsible for the day-to-day communication with the athletes whenever it's required. If there was ever a group of Neanderthals who speak Malenglish at the most rudimentary levels, it's these guys.

In fact, one such guy is holding for my dad on line three right now, and he's apparently pissed off that dad's incommunicado for three weeks on safari in Africa. If he weren't the biggest star in major league baseball and the current Home Run King, I'd probably let him go to my voicemail, but since the last guy who did that is now working at Krystal taking orders for chili cheese pups and fries, I'm going to take the call.

Chapter 3

The Argonne Forest, France
October, 1918

Hail Mary, Full of Grace, The Lord is with thee.
Blessed art thou among women,
and blessed is the fruit of thy womb, Jesus.
Holy Mary, Mother of God, pray for us sinners now,
and at the hour of death. Amen.

It was times like this when Sergeant Joe Marinolli of
the 77th Infantry Division was glad that he had been brought
up in a Roman Catholic orphanage, because saying a hundred
Hail Mary's was the only thing that could save him now.
Major Whittlesey had sent word to every foxhole that the
German troops had them surrounded, but that surrender was

not an option. Joey hadn't been real big on praying as a teenager at the orphanage, but now he would give or do anything for one last chance to see his wife and baby boy, Joey Jr.

The Army had seemed like a logical choice for an eighteen year-old boy with no family and no formal education, so Joe had enlisted in 1912 on the very day that he left the orphanage. The world was at peace at the time, so Joe never pictured being sent to France for hand-to-hand combat. He had simply seen the military as an opportunity to gain some stability in his life and to forge a career that others would respect. His hard work ethic and street sense had paid off, and Joe had been promoted at every opportunity.

By 1915, Joe had met and married a civilian waitress named Rose Peterson, and for the first time since losing his parents almost a decade earlier, Joe was part of a real family again. The Peterson clan hailed from Boston, and they welcomed Joe into their family like a son. Rose and Joe lived in military housing on the base, and by the summer of 1917, they were ready to start trying for children of their own.

Apparently the Marinolli family's run of good fortune was still going strong, because Rose became pregnant right away and by March of 1918, Joe Marinolli, Jr. was born. He was the spitting image of his father, and Joe spent every waking moment holding his son and dreaming of the day when he could teach Joey to play baseball, just like his father had taught him so long ago.

Joe's memories of his father had started to fade, but he could still see clearly the nights that his father and he had spent talking baseball with Frank Bowerman over root beers and cookies. What he would give to be back there now instead of hunkering down in this fox hole waiting to kill or be killed by German soldiers.

As the memories of Frank Bowerman and the "great baseball card heist" came back to him, Joe had to chuckle. He had essentially survived off of those cards during the remainder of his stay at the orphanage -- using them as a precious commodity that could be bartered for anything from candy to clothes -- and all because of another random stroke of good luck that he had discovered later that night.

As it turned out, when Joe had finally gotten around to opening the cardboard box in his room after everyone else was asleep, the contents were not exactly what he had expected. He had been correct about there being a hundred uncut sheets of cards in the box, and he had been right about the sheet having five cards across and six down. But he was wrong in thinking that each sheet would contain only Frank Bowerman cards.

The reason that Joe had seen nothing but Bowerman cards through the opening in the top of the box was because Bowerman was the middle card on the sheet running vertically, so the gap between the flaps lined up perfectly with the six images of Bowerman one atop the other. When Joe had finally opened the flaps that night, he was astonished to see that there were actually five different players pictured horizontally across the sheet, with each player's image repeated vertically a total of six times like so:

A B C D E
A B C D E
A B C D E
A B C D E
A B C D E
A B C D E

Whereas Joe had seen Bowerman's card in the middle or "C" position, it was the player pictured in the "D" position on each sheet who had turned Little Joey Marinolli into the John D. Rockefeller of the New York Foundling Orphanage. As luck would have it, that player turned out to be none other than the winningest pitcher in the history of professional baseball -- Denton True Young – otherwise known as "Cy" Young.

Joe could still remember the guilt he felt upon making this discovery, both for stealing a box of cards that *did* have some serious value and for being more excited about having six hundred Cy Young cards than he had been about owning three thousand Frank Bowerman cards.

But Joe Marinolli soon realized that he now had the best of both worlds because he could cut up the sheets and trade off the Cy Young cards one at a time while still keeping all of the Frank Bowerman cards for himself. Nobody in his right mind would trade anything for a Bowerman, but a Young? Joe might as well have stolen a case of uncut dollar bills straight from the mint!

By the time he left the orphanage and enlisted in the Army, Trader Joe was out of capital. All he had left in his chest from his original cache were 594 individual cards of Frank Bowerman (which had indeed turned out to be worthless as trade bait) and one remaining uncut sheet that he had purposely left full and intact in pristine condition as a permanent reminder to him of all the joy that Frank Bowerman had brought him at different times in his life.

That final uncut sheet of cards, along with all the other junk he had kept from the orphanage, was now sitting in his locked trunk in the garage of his home back in the states, gathering cobwebs. Joe had purposely never opened the chest for Rose because he didn't want her to see how meager his belongings had been, nor did he want to tell her the truth about how he had come into possession of the cards.

He had vowed never to steal again that night at the orphanage as he said his prayers, and he had stayed true to his word. Now Joe was praying once again, but this time for his life.

As he said his Hail Mary's, Joe thought about those baseball cards -- the only material link joining him, his father and his son -- and he prayed that his decade of good fortune would continue long enough to let him return home alive and some day explain to Joey Jr. the significance of the "Bowerman Treasure."

And as the bullet pierced his chest and exploded his heart, the last vision Sergeant Joe Marinolli saw was his late mother and father, now perfectly hale and hearty again, beckoning with open arms for him to come join them.

Chapter 4

Atlanta
2007

"Hey, Big Stick, this is Chuck," I said as I picked up the phone from behind my desk and logged off of the Gator Country website to which I was addicted. Some people need crack or crystal meth; I just need my sports update every ten minutes. Otherwise, I might go down the hall to make copies and not be fully prepared for a chance encounter with another Malenglish speaking colleague. You never want to be the guy who has to ask someone *else* for a score or a statistic. In that way, I guess it really *isn't* any different than illegal drugs: suppliers are more important than users.

"What can I do for you?" I ask Johns. "You guys got a road trip coming through here any time soon? You need me to hook you back up with that girl from last time, the one with your name tattooed on her breast?"

"Naw, man, she's probably got six guys' names tattooed above mine by now," laughed Jerry Johns, the player known worldwide to baseball fans as The Big Stick. "Can you imagine that? Her tits are the only place in the world where I'm penciled in *seventh* in the freakin' line up!"

I laughed cautiously, hoping that my client had taken steps not to leave a "Little Stick" behind, or else we'd be hearing from her about child support out the ying yang.

"So what's up then?" I asked.

"You tell me what's up? What's this B.S. about your old man being out of the country for three weeks? Why the hell didn't he tell me he was going out of town?"

I choked back a number of smartass comments before finally replying.

"You know he wouldn't have left town if you had anything scheduled like an interview or a commercial being filmed. I know for a fact he double checked this before he left," I said calmly.

Apparently this wasn't enough to pacify him.

"Yeah, well I pay ya'll a boatload of money to take care of whatever I need, and right now I need something really important. What the hell am I supposed to do, go hire another agent for this month?"

The thought of being the one at the firm responsible for losing our biggest client had me already smelling Krystal burgers on the grill.

"Look, just tell me what you need, and you know I'm good for it," I pleaded. "What do you need, a cup of hot fat and the head of Alfredo Garcia?"

"Don't be spouting off no *Fletch* to me right now or you'll be sleeping out on the street like Fat Sam and Gummy," he growled. "Did you read the damn *USA Today* today?"

"The *USA Today* today? Now you sound like Lou Gehrig's famous speech with that echo in the background," I said, still trying to loosen him up a bit. "No, I haven't read it yet. What's up, is there another article trying to link you to steroids? Just give me the writer's name and we'll have him sued by this afternoon."

"No, I'm past all that crap. Let 'em say whatever the hell they want, I can't stop 'em from guessing. The only thing I can do is go pull my pants down on national TV and say 'These look like shrunken raisins to you?' but I don't think the commissioner would like that too much, do you?"

"No, I don't," I replied, thinking to myself that we'd already handled three confidential paternity suits for Johns. If word of those settlements ever leaked out, there'd be nobody in the media questioning his testicular capability. He just wasn't the type who wanted to settle down, as the song says,

"Papa Was a Rolling Stone" – The Temptations, 1972

"Well, you need to go get a copy of the paper," Johns continued, "because there's a big story on the front page about a baseball card that just sold for $2,500,000…and I'm wondering how come that card isn't in *my* possession right now? Isn't that what I hire you guys to do?"

Over the years, our firm had indeed controlled all of Stickman's investment opportunities, putting his twenty million dollar annual salary to work for him in a number of diverse areas. Because of these solid investments, his net worth (after the paternity suits, his forty-five silk suits and the IRS men in grey suits) was still somewhere north of

$175,000,000. If he had only been more charismatic, we probably could have tripled those numbers with more commercial endorsements.

"Stick, you pay us to take care of your money, and you know we've done you right. I don't know the first thing about baseball cards, but if I had opened the paper this morning and found out that a member of our firm had spent that much of our client's money on a little piece of cardboard, I would have called our malpractice carrier and told them to get the checkbook ready."

"I know Chuck, I hear you loud and clear, but this card is apparently a big deal. How about all these ugly paintings you guys made me buy and put on the walls -- these stupid things that are just one solid color on top and another on the bottom. I've got twenty guys on my team that can paint better than this crap. What are these things worth now?"

I had to laugh to myself at the Stickman's description of his authentic Rothko originals. I never really understood the attraction to them either, but apparently someone else really does.

"Those are Mark Rothkos, Stick, and based on the latest auction results, I would guess that yours are now worth about a cool fifteen million altogether. *They're gold, Jerry, gold!*"

"Oh yeah, if they're so gold, what did I pay for 'em two years ago?"

I tried to remember. "I'm pretty sure it was about ten million -- and them's not 1954 dollars -- so I'd say they've gone up right around fifty percent in a little over two years."

He paused for a minute before he got it. "*Raising Arizona*, right? The part where the bounty hunter's talking about how much he was worth as a kid?"

I smiled to myself, knowing how easy it had been to lure Jerry into some Malenglish banter by throwing him a slow-pitch softball and letting him think he's hit my best pitch. "Yeah, you're good. That's a tough one."

Stick chuckled before getting back on track. "Chuck, this damn baseball card sold for $2,500,000 last week, and the guy that sold it had bought it only two years earlier for *half* that much. The thing *doubled* in value while these stupid paintings were stuck in second gear!"

I was dumbfounded. Was there really money to be made in *baseball cards*? As I was beginning to really spin the concept around in my head, the Stick broke the silence.

"Did you hear me Chuck? Now you see why I'm so pissed off? I'm the best baseball player in the world, so if anyone deserves to own the best baseball card in the world, it's me.

Maybe I need to put it in a way that you'll understand: you remember that part in *Raising Arizona* where she tells him to go back in there and get her a baby?"

"Yeah," I heard myself say weakly.

"Well, I want me a baseball card, so you go out there and get me that card, Chuck! If you don't, I'll get me a new agent – or my name's not Jerry Johns!"

He slammed down the phone so hard it left a ringing in my ear. Okay, where does one go to find the world's most expensive baseball card? Tiffany & Co.? Or better yet: Cardier?

I kill myself; really, I do.

Chapter 5

Atlanta
2007

After sitting in shock for a few more minutes, I snapped out of my funk and gathered up two of the firm's young associates for an important business lunch. I grabbed the two guys who know the most about baseball, Jim Jefferson (picture Denzel Washington) and Alex Preston (picture the whole state of Washington) and filled them in on our new assignment over burgers and fries.

"I can't believe this happened while your dad is gone. You picked the wrong week to quit sniffing glue, man," said Alex, who knew every line from *Airplane!* including the parts spoken in jive.

He'd graduated in the top five percent of his class at Duke, but that didn't earn him a fraction of the respect from his peers that his mastery of Leslie Neilsen films did. If you have to go on-line and do a search to find out what the translation of s*ee a broad to get that booty yak 'em...leg 'er down 'n smack 'em yak 'em* is, then you aren't in his league. (Hint: Think Benjamin Frankin)

"Tell me about it," I replied, hearing a familiar old song come on through the speakers in the ceiling. "How appropriate; *Rock Me Gently,*" I said, pointing to the speaker. "I could use some TLC right now. Who sings it?"

They both mulled it over while chewing a mouthful of fries; Alex's mouthful containing about five times as many as Jim's.

"Some lame white guy, that's for sure. Was it Shawn Cassidy?" Jim asked.

"Nah, he was *Da Doo Ron Ron.*"

Alex had no clue, but he knew that the rules of proper Malenglish required him to give it a shot. "Bay City Rollers?" he managed to get out while scarfing down half of his burger in one bite.

I smiled at having stumped them both, even though it wasn't really fair since they were a few years younger than I was. "No, they did *Saturday Night.* It's Andy Kim. A definite one-hit wonder, which is why it's such a toughie."

"I wonder how much money a guy like that has made in his lifetime from that one song?" Jim posed. "He's got a huge hit record that everyone in the world has heard a hundred times, but I wonder if he could even afford to own this crazy baseball card we're talking about?"

"I doubt it," Alex said while wiping the ketchup off his face with his napkin.

"Whether *he* can or not doesn't matter," I said glumly. "What matters is that *Jerry Johns* can afford it, so we need to get started researching this damn thing to find out who owns it and whether or not it's a legitimate investment vehicle."

They both nodded their heads as I continued.

"Jim, you get in touch with our contacts at the auction houses where we sell our clients' game-used jerseys and bats. We funnel so much business to those guys that they owe us big time. Squeeze them to find out the real story behind the sale and the identity of the new owner.

Alex, I need you to get on-line and find out everything you can about the history of this card and the collecting community. Before we can spend a dime on this thing, we've got to make sure it's the real deal."

"You got it," they said in unison, as the waitress delivered our desert orders to the table. You don't eat a meal with Alex without getting dessert. It would be like letting an alcoholic drink alone, because he's going to get one whether you do or not. I took a bite of my Chocolate Sin cake and felt my troubles melting away. Sure it would force me to do an extra twenty minutes on the treadmill that night, but I was in serious need of some "comfort food" and this was hitting the spot.

"You think this is what the Starland Vocal Band was singing about?" I asked.

Alex smiled wickedly and responded, "Yeah, but I liked Ron Burgundy and the Channel 4 News Team's version better."

Jim had been completely lost until Alex's *Anchorman* allusion. He exhaled a sigh of relief, knowing that he was now safe, since failing to know any Will Ferrell quote would have been grounds for expulsion from any Malenglish-speaking society.

By the way, if I failed to mention it earlier, there is a simple alkaline test to use in determining whether or not someone speaks Malenglish. You merely wait for the appropriate time and then declare: *"Over? It can't be over. Was it over when the Germans bombed Pearl Harbor?"*

If they stare at you with confusion or try to correct you and point out that it was the Japanese who bombed Pearl Harbor, you know that you're wasting your time trying to carry on a conversation with that individual. Odds are the person is a female, but occasionally you will encounter the rare someone with a Y chromosome who doesn't give the proper retort. These are the scary ones, because they may look normal on the outside, but inside their wires are all crossed. They most likely prefer *Entertainment Tonight* to *SportsCenter*, so consider yourself forewarned should you try to bond with one of these Malenglish-challenged males.

No, the only acceptable response to the Malenglish test, of course, would be the next line from Animal House: *"Don't stop him; he's on a roll."*

"Starland Vocal Band: *Afternoon Delight*," Jim finally said with a smile, taking another big bite of his desert. "I doubt they were talking about chocolate cake, though."

"Probably not," Alex agreed, "but at my size, it's a lot easier to find cake than sex -- and cheaper, too!"

With that, the three of us headed back to the office to try and find out everything we could about a baseball card – excuse me – *the* baseball card. What on earth was so special about *this* card and why does everybody want it?

"Everybody Wants You" – Billy Squier, 1982.

Chapter 6

Boston
December, 1943

Rose Marinolli had spent the past twenty years cursing polio for what it had done to her son, and now she spent her every waking moment thanking God for the unforeseen blessing that He'd bestowed upon her when little Joey had been stricken with polio at age five.

It had been a difficult struggle as a widow and single parent to survive the Great Depression with a young cripple who was unable to give much assistance around the house, but those same leg braces that were the butt of many jokes were now the lifesaving devices preventing her son from joining the Army and following in his late father's footsteps. Rose has already lost one half of her heart to the Germans; losing the other half in the same manner was unthinkable.

But with her son safely home stateside, Rose had thrown herself full throttle into the war effort. She was a volunteer leader at the local USO, giving countless hours of her time to do anything she could to help our boys overseas get revenge for the loss of her husband. Not a day went by that she didn't think of Joey Sr.; the image of him as a twenty-four year old soldier still burned in her mind.

Even though Joey Jr. was already older than his dad had been at his death, she was never able to picture them as father and son. To her, they were more like long lost brothers who had never met.

The difference between the two, however, was night and day. Where Joey Sr. had been outgoing and physically gifted, Joey Jr. was shy and withdrawn; he was more interested in reading a book than going outdoors. Certainly growing up with the aftereffects of polio had made him this way.

Had his father been alive, Rose was convinced that he could have helped Joey become at least a fan of outdoor sports if not a participant. As it was, however, all Joey Jr. knew about baseball was that in his lifetime, neither of the local Boston teams had ever made it to the World Series. Therefore, he figured he really wasn't missing anything special anyway.

The latest project that Rose had become engrossed in was chairing the USO paper and rubber recycling drive in her neighborhood. The war had already pushed on for much longer than anyone had expected it would, and resources were becoming scarce. Food rationing had taken a toll on morale throughout the city, but Rose was dead set on making sure that everybody understood the importance of the efforts and contributed to the cause.

This meant, of course, that Rose was going to donate anything in her house that was made of paper or rubber and wasn't nailed down -- including any old keepsakes of Joey Sr. After all, she was doing this in his honor and she knew that he would want it that way.

So as much as it pained her to think about parting with it, Rose knew that she had to find her husband's old rubber basketball in the basement and give it to the drive. Joey Jr. had definitely never used it, so she knew that it had to still be stored somewhere down in the basement where all the rest of her husband's old belongings were kept. Rose had never been able to bring herself to throw any of his stuff away, but neither had she ever been able to get the courage to really go through his things and inventory them. The painful recollections that they triggered just made it too much to bear.

As she made her way down the stairs and found the basketball hidden on a shelf behind some canned goods, she noticed her husband's old footlocker with "*Property of New York Foundling*" printed on the side. She knew that he had brought this with him into their marriage from his days at the orphanage, but she had never seen him open it or even make reference to what was inside.

She had asked him once what was inside the trunk, but he simply laughed and quoted the old proverb about one man's trash being another man's treasure. He assured her that nothing in the trunk would ever be worth more than the trunk itself, so she had never paid it another minute of thought. Until now.

What was in there? What if it was something that she could donate to the war effort? Whatever it was, it was from a time in his life before the two of them had ever met, so she wasn't too worried about finding anything that would unleash a torrent of sad emotions that she couldn't handle. Or was she?

"Joey, can you please come down here a minute, sweetheart? I need your help with something."

"Sure, Mom, be right there," he yelled.

As Joey limped down the stairs, holding the handrails for support, she told him what she wanted to do.

"Are you sure, Mom? There's probably nothing in there now but old clothes or toys that nobody would want. If Dad had brought anything important with him from the orphanage, wouldn't he have given it to you before he died?"

"Probably," she said, "but then again, he didn't know there would be a recycling drive going on. If there is just one thing in there that helps us win this war and beat the Germans, then he would be the first to give it away."

Joey had come over and eyed the chest, and then walked over to the workbench to grab an old pair of bolt cutters. He got himself into position to cut the padlock and then hesitated.

"Any guesses?" he asked with a quizzical look on his face.

"Your father never talked much about his stay in the orphanage and even less about his childhood before his parents died, so it could be anything."

"Well," said Joey, snapping the lock, "let's hope that he somehow came across a stash of gold bearer bonds and was just saving them here for a rainy day."

He wiped the heavy layer of dust of the lid of the trunk and opened it.

"Well, I know that the pen is mightier than the sword, but I doubt that these will help us kill any Nazis," Joey quipped.

Rose leaned over to look. The chest was full of old newspapers; the sports sections to be precise. She could see where Joey Sr. had made notations around the box score of a New York Giants game in 1911, scribbling tidbits to himself in pencil and calculating batting averages for certain players in the margins. Apparently, from the bulk of the contents, he had done so every day for several years.

"Did you know that Dad loved baseball *this* much?"

"Yes, he used to tell me that it was his first love. I know that was something he had gotten from his father before he died, so I knew it was his way of trying to hold onto that connection."

Rose began digging through the yellowed papers, making sure that there was nothing else in the crate. Once she had removed enough of them, she could see that the only other thing inside was an old felt blanket lining the bottom. No sense in emptying the locker, she thought to herself, when she could use it to carry the newspapers and have someone take the whole thing down to the USO.

"I'll just call Mr. Henry and have him and his son come over here and load this onto their truck," she told Joey. "They can carry it down to the center and maybe they will have some use for the trunk after the papers are recycled."

"Mom," Joey said softly with a somber look on his face, "I really don't have anything to remember Dad by, so do you think maybe we could just donate the papers and let me keep the trunk? I could use it to store my old toys and stuff from when I was kid that are just sitting under my bed right now. I'll just bring it back down here to the basement when I'm done."

"Sure Honey, I think that's a great idea," said Rose, wiping away a tear. "Let's just empty out these papers and stack them up right here. Once it's empty, I think the two of us will be able to get it up the stairs."

They began unloading the piles, pausing occasionally to read one of the articles or trying to decipher the faded shorthand scribbles of a teenage Joey Marinolli Sr.

"Apparently 1911 and 1912 were good years for the New York Giants," Joey noted as he flipped through the pages. "They went to the World Series both years, but lost both times."

"Hey, look at this!" he exclaimed, pulling one particular issue of the New York Times out from the bottom of the stack. "This is pretty neat. Turns out it was the Red Sox who beat the Giants and won the championship in 1912. I'll bet some of the big Red Sox fans here in town might pay good money for a souvenir like this!"

"Your father is probably rolling over in his grave at the thought of us profiting off of his beloved team's misery," Rose chuckled. "I doubt anyone will give you two cents for it, but you go right ahead and try. In fact, knowing your father, that's the kind of creative ingenuity he would have liked."

Joey grinned at the thought of making his dad proud. He finished getting the rest of the papers out and then noticed something at the bottom of the crate. Resting on top of the blanket, spread all over, were hundreds and hundreds of little colored drawings.

"What are these?" he asked, grabbing a handful and handing them to his mother.

"I don't have any idea. Apparently your father was a big fan of this Bowerman person. Are they all of him?"

Joey spread all the cards around inside the box, mixing them up so that he could see them all.

"Yeah, they all have the same picture on front -- this Bowerman guy. And it says that he played for Boston. Why would dad care about a Boston player?"

"I don't have any idea," said Rose, who was truly puzzled and trying to unravel the mystery in her head. "I know that your father had never been to Boston before we met. I can't begin to understand what interest he would have had with this Bowerman fellow."

Joey turned one of the cards over and read aloud from the back:

"Baseball Series, 150 subjects; Piedmont, the Cigarette of Quality."

He turned to Rose and raised an eyebrow.

"Did dad ever smoke? Maybe he just smoked this one brand and the only player's card that came with that brand was this one?"

"No, that can't be it. He never smoked in the years that I knew him, and I seriously doubt that he could have afforded to smoke when he was growing up in the orphanage. From hearing him talk, it was all he could do to get food in his belly."

Joey started gathering up the curious little cards and stacking them into piles.

"Well," he said, "if I can find someone who will buy that old newspaper about the Red Sox, then maybe I can find someone who might buy these old Boston cards as well. If I can't, then we can just donate them to the Y.M.C.A. and they can give them out to the kids."

Soon the crate was empty with no further surprises revealed. In a way, Rose was relieved that they hadn't discovered any dark secret from her husband's past that would tarnish her memory of him in any way.

"Just leave that piece of cloth in the bottom to provide some cushion for your toys."

"OK, good idea, Mom."

Joey closed the lid and grabbed one of the side handles. "This thing doesn't weigh hardly anything now, so let's see if we can get it up to my room together."

Sure enough, the two of them were able to hoist the empty footlocker and make it back up the stairs with no problem. They found an empty space in the back of the hall closet, and Joey went to his room to start reloading the crate with his own version of "another man's treasure."

A few minutes later he finished the task and closed the lid.

"Just think, Joey. Maybe someday you can find someone special and provide me with some grandkids of my own. Then we can all come back here and drag this crate out and let your kids see what you collected," Rose said in a half-joking tone. In her heart, however, she was concerned that this might never come to fruition.

Joey was embarrassed by this subject and his lack of prowess with members of the opposite sex, and Rose could tell that she had hurt his feelings.

"I will Mom, I promise," he stammered.

But then he brightened up and cracked, "Who knows, maybe this Bowerman guy was the best baseball player ever? Maybe these cards are worth so much that the ladies will be knocking down our door to marry me?"

Rose laughed out loud and gave her son a big hug. "Who would ever pay good money for old junk?"

Chapter 7

Atlanta
2007

Alex and Jim were sitting on my couch enjoying the Fellini's pizzas and cold Red Brick Ales that I had promised them if they would come over after work with their research to fill me in on their findings. Like a mule will chase the carrot on a stick out in from of him for days on end and a mole will come out of his dark habitat for feeding purposes, a male will do both for pizza and beer. Not much of a difference between the three creatures really, just interchange a vowel here or there.

"Who's the only big leaguer to ever throw back-to-back no hitters," Jim asked, obviously having done some research before coming over in hopes of retaining his crown from lunch.

"Johnny Vander Meer," Alex said without missing a beat. "Way too easy. Who was the only big leaguer to pitch a perfect game for twelve innings and then lose the game in the thirteenth?"

"Harvey Haddix, Pittsburgh Pirates, 1959," I answered correctly. "Do you think he had some words for his teammates after the game or what? The guy goes out and shuts down Hank Aaron and the mighty Braves for twelve innings with nobody reaching base, and his teammates can't score one damn run for him. In this day and age, a guy would go on ESPN and demand a trade if that happened to him."

"Wouldn't that be *our* job?" Jim said half-jokingly. "What good agent would let his client suffer like that? I'd have also filed a lawsuit for lack of support. Think of how much leverage we would have lost in contract negations when our client lost his bid for a perfect game."

"Holy crap," Alex piped up, "do you know who the shortstop was for that 1959 Pirates team? Dick Groat! Remember that episode of *Curb Your Enthusiasm*? The one where Larry gets in a fight with the hyperactive kid with Groat's Syndrome?"

"Yeah! Larry thought the disease was named after the old Pirates' shortstop," I exclaimed. "But do you remember the most classic part of that episode?"

Alex nods his head rapidly, trying desperately to swallow his pizza so that he can get his response in before the buzzer. "Yeah, that weirdo wins 'Lunch with Larry' at the charity auction, and then when Larry's appetizer arrives first and Larry asks him rhetorically if the guy minds whether he starts eating without him, the guy makes a stink and says, yes, he minds because he'd paid for lunch with Larry and didn't want to be cheated."

"Hey, he was just being honest," Jim said. "Inappropriate as hell, but brutally honest. If you think about it, Larry would have done the same thing if he had paid for a lunch with Ted Danson or someone like that."

We all agreed and took a big swig of our beers. The only thing left in the pizza box was a tiny half-eaten slice of pie and the little white plastic thingamabob that holds the lids of the box up and keeps it from crushing the pizza. It dawned on me that I may have just hit the mother lode.

"Okay, smart guys, what is this thing called?" I asked, picking up the three-legged piece of plastic and tossing it to Alex.

"It's called a 'pizza saver' and there is actually a patent on the thing," said Alex, swatting it out of the air with his palm and knocking it across the room. "Goodbye Mr. Spalding!" he bellowed as he pumped his fist like Kirk Gibson.

"Oh, he got all of that one," Jim added in his best Carl Spackler. "He's *gotta* be pleased with that one."

"Anybody want to finish of this last piece?" I asked.

"No way, man, I'm stuffed," Alex said, puffing out his already puffy cheeks.

"It's *wafer* thin," I added in a Monty Python accent.

Jim softly began the chant from the famous pie-eating contest in *Stand By Me*: "Lardass…lardass…lardass…"

"All right, all right, give me the damn thing!" Alex laughed as he wolfed it down like a vacuum hose sucking up a crumb. You did *not* want to get anywhere near Alex's mouth at feeding time.

I threw the empty pizza box in the trash can and got down to business. "All right Jim, what's the word on the street about this card? Did you talk to our folks at the auction houses?"

"Yep, and here's what I've got so far. I called the auction house that sold the card and talked to a guy I know in the appraisal division. He wouldn't tell me who bought the card, since confidentiality is the cornerstone of their whole operation, but he promised that he would put me in touch with the 'bidding agent' for the buyer.

Apparently the buyer wanted to remain anonymous, so he paid someone to be present and bid on his behalf. That's the guy who the auction house put me in touch with, Barry Stone up in Brooklyn. Apparently Stone's a dinosaur in the hobby and one of the few card dealers out there who's on the up-and-up."

Jim paused to take a sip of his beer and to check his notes before continuing. "So Stone finally calls me, and since I knew that he wouldn't reveal his client, I had prepared a message for him to pass on to his source. I let Stone know that I was calling on behalf of Jerry "Big Stick" Johns, and that we were interested in talking about a deal for the card that would include some quid-pro-quo on our end, like a bunch of signed game-used memorabilia from the Johns himself.

I know I probably should have checked with you first before doing this, Chuck, but I had a hunch that I wanted to play. I figured anybody who would spend that much on a baseball card was a real freak of a fan, so I thought the lure of meeting the Big Stick in person would be very tempting."

I shrugged my shoulders. "I think it was a great idea on your part. I'm just not sure Stickman is going to like having to spend time with some pencil-necked jock-sniffer."

"I know, I thought about that," Jim said, "but I figure he'll do it if we tell him how much it will save him off the price of the card. Plus, he normally has to pay income taxes on all of his gains from memorabilia sales, whereas this way he can get credit for full value for his things with the in-kind trade we do on the card."

"Makes sense," Alex agreed.

"So anyway, I told this Stone guy about our representation of Stickman and how we would be willing to work out a trade for the card plus some amount of cash, and of course he starts talking about how his client would never want to part with it, has always dreamed about owning it, can't imagine living without it, yada, yada, yada. I had to remind him that we negotiate contracts on a daily basis against the owners of every major sports franchise, so we really don't need to hear any of his puffery."

"Go on," I said to Jim.

"I also reminded him of how much the Big Stick's famous home run bat sold for at auction and how his client would be getting stuff like that in return for the card, and I think I got him convinced that he might even get a little something as a cut for making the deal work. He said he would talk to the client and get back to me soon. He didn't call me back today, and I don't want to call him back and look desperate, so I'll give him a day or two and then see where it stands."

"Good job," I said with sincerity. "I think what we need to do from here if they are interested is let me take over the negotiations and come in from scratch as the 'bad cop' who isn't sold on the deal. That way we can turn the tables and hopefully get them begging us to make the swap."

"That's cool with me. You're the one who's safe around the office. The last thing I need is to be known around town as the dumb black kid who spent millions of dollars on a baseball card of some old white guy. There's no street cred in that at all," Jim said, holding his fingers cocked out in front of his body pantomiming some gang's hand gesture.

"Ha!" Alex chimed in, "you lost any chance at street cred when you bought that Volvo last year, Holmes! You're more white bread than Eddie Murphy was in that skit where he walked around like a honky. 'What are you doing? I'm buying this newspaper. Go ahead, take it – there's nobody around'!"

"He's right Jim," I laughed out loud. "Nobody's going to confuse you for Tyrone Green anytime soon. 'Kill my landlord. Kill my landlord.'"

By now Jim was laughing so hard he had to hold his nose to keep from snorting out his beer. "Okay, Okay," he finally said. "Regardless of my race, creed or religion, I'm still glad that you'll be the one handling the deal, Chuck. I'd feel too much like the black sheriff on *Blazing Saddles* if you left me with all that pressure."

"Good," I stated, "then you just let me know when he calls you back and I'll go from there. Assuming, that is, that Alex here is able to bring me up to speed on what the hell is so special about this baseball card. I'm assuming it's old and rare, but there's got to be more to it than that, right Alex?"

"Way more, guys," Alex stated proudly. "This baby is the Holy Grail of the entire sports memorabilia market!"

"African or European?" I snipped.

"I fart in your general direction," Alex said without pausing, picking up adroitly on my Malenglish quip and then hoisting me with my own petard.

Alex continued. "The ironic thing is that it's not the oldest card nor is it the rarest card. It's just the one card that everyone in the hobby knows about and wants to own; it has always been thus. It's far more popular than the second largest ball of twine on the face of the earth or any other totally worthless collectible item that's value is 100% intrinsic."

Alex started thumbing through his papers and pulled out a color copy enlargement of the card that he had printed off the internet.

"Here's the card itself, a 1909 card of Honus Wagner from the set known as T-206. The "T" stands for "Tobacco" because these cards came in packs of cigarettes distributed by the American Tobacco Company between 1909 and 1911. Now Wagner was definitely one of the best players in the game at the time, but that's not why his cards are so valuable.

In fact, Wagner has dozens of other cards in other sets that aren't worth any more than a hundred bucks or so. No, the reason this card is so valuable is because the T-206 set is a very popular set for collectors to try and complete, and to complete your set, you have to have a Honus Wagner card."

"Okay," Jim interrupted him, "but wouldn't that be true for *every* player? In other words, you couldn't complete the set without a Billy Barue card either."

"Ah," Alex grinned, "that's the key to this whole mess. For some reason -- some think because he disliked cigarettes and others say because he wasn't getting paid enough for the use of his picture -- Honus Wagner wrote to an agent for the company in 1909 and specifically asked them *not* to use his image on any of their cards.

He even went so far as to pay the agent back for the fee that the agent would have received if he had procured Wagner's approval. So that's why almost every other card from the set still exists today in fairly large numbers, yet the Wagner is extremely rare. Only about fifty or so are thought to still exist."

"But why do any exist *at all* if he told them not to use his likeness on their cards?" I asked.

"Nobody knows for sure, of course, but the obvious answer is that the factory printing the cards had already prepared their printing presses and had produced a small amount of them before they got the word to stop producing them. Nobody knows if the ones that survived were ever actually inserted into pack of cigarettes or whether they were just saved as scraps and cut up later.

And speaking of cutting, it is apparently a mortal sin to use scissors to trim the edges of a baseball card. You would think that people would do it all the time to make old ratty cards look sharper, but doing so can decrease the value of a card 90%."

"Good Lord," I muttered. "How would anyone ever know if a card has been trimmed microscopically or maybe was just a counterfeit altogether? For $2,500,000, you would think that people would be printing these things off like advertising flyers!"

"Well, it's funny you should say that," Alex said as he pulled another bundle of papers from his folder. "Here are all the current ebay auctions for a T-206 Honus Wagner card. As you can see, there are currently 658 up for auction, with the lowest one starting at ninety-nine cents. Obviously people *are* printing them off on their laser printers at home and trying to con people with them, so the authenticity and pedigree of any valuable card is an absolute must.

"Oh great," I said warily.

"Don't worry," Alex continued, "that's why there are certain companies out there who hire the best experts in vintage paper composition, vintage printing press procedures, vintage ink dating measures and so forth. The *only* way to get any real money for your card, whether it's a Honus Wagner or a Billy Barue, is to have it certified by these companies. They permanently seal it in an airtight plastic slab and assign it a computer bar code number; once they do this, it's almost as liquid on the market as cash itself."

"So I guess we can assume that this one was certified, huh?" Jim asked.

"You bet, and that's another whole level of the mystery behind this one particular card. You remember I said that there are about fifty of these T-206 Wagner cards still out there in various locations, right? Well, all fifty of them vary in condition from very, very crappy to near mint. The last really tattered one sold at auction in February for $150,000.

In contrast, you have the one that just sold for $2,500,000, which only fetched that much because it is the absolute best-known example of the card that still exists. Look at the picture. It's almost a hundred years old but it still has sharp corners and no creases. Whoever bought it clearly wanted nothing but the best, because this one is head and shoulders better than even the next-best one known to exist, which has sold in the past for somewhere close to $500,000."

"It shows on this picture that it graded an '8' on a scale of what, one to ten?" I asked.

"Yep," Alex answered. "I looked to see if any company had grades that went up to eleven, so their cards would be one better, but apparently there aren't many *Spinal Tap* fans in the baseball grading business."

"Hold on a minute," Jim said quickly, sitting up and looking back through his own notes. "Mr. Stone mentioned to me that he could get his hands on another T-206 Wagner for us for a much better price, so this grading scale difference is probably what he was referring to. If we can find one of these cards for Jerry Johns that's a '1' or a '2' and falls in the $200,000 range, then the Stick will think we hung the moon! Hell, he won't have to do anything but donate a signed bat and a signed hat for that amount!"

"Well, there's one more thing I need to mention, and I have no idea whether it matters to Johns or not," Alex stated.

"The one other reason why this particular card sold for such a large amount is because it has a rare back. Of the fifty or so certified T-206 Wagners that are known to exist, all but about two of them have the "Sweet Caporal" cigarette brand advertisement on the back. Apparently someone at that factory didn't get the word in time to stop them from getting shipped out."

"Interesting," Jim noted.

"But the other two, which are the rarest of the rare, have the "Piedmont" cigarette brand back. Nobody even knew that a Wagner card existed with this back until the 1950's when a collector named Charles Bray said that he had heard about one and was trying to purchase it. That one was in average condition from what I understand, so it was not the one that just sold.

Apparently this $2,500,000 card showed up for the first time at a flea market in Florida in the early 1980's. It was bought by someone from New York, and then reportedly resold by that person in 1985 for only $25,000," Alex concluded.

"God, why couldn't I have bought the damn thing back then?" Jim sighed. "I could be the one holding a card that had appreciated a *hundred times* its value in only about twenty years!"

"Okay boys, I think our work here tonight is done," I said, clicking off the mute button so that we could now hear the whiny voice of Skip Caray calling the action of the Braves game that we had been watching with the sound off. "I'll call Stick in the morning, explain the situation to him, and let him decide what he wants to do. I'll tell him that he can get a nice example of one without the rare back for about $200,000, and the firm will have once again made peace with our most famous client. I'll be sure to let my dad know how much you guys helped out."

I could tell how much that meant to the guys since they were still trying to climb the ladder and become partners in the firm. Hopefully my dad would make it back from Africa alive so that I really could talk to him on their behalf. For all I knew, he'd already been gored by a rhino or eaten by a tribe of Bushmen worshipping a Coke bottle.

Chapter 8

New York City
Winter, 1970

Still stinging from the grief of having to bury his mother and best friend of 52 years, Joey -- now Dr. Joe Marinolli, Jr. -- knew that the only people he could count on to get him out of his depression were his kids; his 179 kids.

No, Joey Jr. had not gone overboard in fulfilling the promise of grandchildren that he had made to his mother so many years ago. In fact, he had never even married, deciding instead to completely dedicate himself to his passion of books. He had stayed at home in Boston with his mother while completing his postgraduate work at Harvard in the field of rare books and classical literature, practically living in the dark recesses of the school's Houghton Library. It wasn't the largest or most-frequented library on campus, but it was where the rarest books were stored. Since most of the young women in those days had been busy marrying soldiers just returning from the war and not hanging out in gloomy libraries, Joey never really had a chance. He'd accepted his lot in life as an introverted bookworm, and was determined to be the best one that he could be.

So no, none of the 179 kids that Dr. Joe Marinolli was presently thinking about were his biological children, but that didn't make him love them any less. They ranged in age from five to eighteen, equal numbers of boys and girls, and they were the current residents of the New York Foundling Orphanage.

The location of the orphanage had changed since the time Joey's father had been a resident in 1909 -- a new state-of-the art building had been built at the corner of 68th Street and Third Avenue in 1958 -- but the mission was unchanged. And every time Joey came through the front door, he couldn't help but think that he owed his very existence to this facility. If his father had not had the orphanage to help him survive after losing both parents, then his father would have never been alive to sire him. Ergo, "Dr. Joe" as all the children called him owed his life to the New York Foundling; it was a debt he intended to repay in spades.

His initial encounter with the orphanage, however, was more the result of a series of chance happenings than it was a planned event. In 1956, at age 40, Joey had already made quite a name for himself in the field of rare books, and was contacted by the auction house Sotheby's to come in and consult for them on a particular project. A very old private library collection had been bequeathed to the orphanage by a philanthropist who himself had been raised at the New York Foundling as a child, so Dr. Marinolli was called in to document and catalog the collection before it could be auctioned off.

Sotheby's had just opened their New York office a year earlier in 1955, so they were still searching for a rare book expert to whom they could turn on a fairly regular basis. So after pulling some strings, the auction house was able to procure a full-time position for Joey as a curator at the New York Public Library and promised to supply him with enough consulting business in his spare time to make him financially comfortable. Joey accepted the offer and moved his aging mother with him from Boston to Manhattan, but it wasn't the money that made him do it, or even the opportunity to handle some of the most valuable and scarcest works of literature known to man.

It was the kids.

Joey had first met the kids on his initial trip to New York when the people from Sotheby's had taken him by the orphanage to show him where the proceeds for the private library sale would be channeled. The facility at that time was in shambles and severely overcrowded, but morale was high because the prospect of moving to a new building was on the horizon.

They had already broken ground on the new project and had raised enough pledges and donations to finish the project, but it was made clear to Joey that the substantial amount they were expecting to receive from the auction was going to make the difference between these kids eating Spam or real ham for the next several years. The thought of kids going hungry broke Joey's heart, so he accepted the Sotheby's assignment on the spot and dove headfirst into the project.

Ironically, while Joey had a warm spot in his heart because he knew that his own father had been raised in an orphanage, he hadn't remembered the specific name of his father's facility. He knew that he had seen it once stenciled on the side of that old trunk, but he couldn't recall what it said. It wasn't until he returned to Boston and broke the news of his new assignment to his mother that the puzzle was solved.

"The New York Foundling!" Rose exclaimed with shock. "You actually *went* there? Don't you know that that's where your father spent his teenage years?"

"Oh my God," Joey gasped, as the significance of his visit to the facility finally sank in. "You're right! *That's* the name on the side of his old trunk. Wow, I hope it was a little nicer when Dad was a kid. It's practically falling down now."

"Well, it sounds like you can do something about that," Rose said proudly. "You're going to take that job and we're going to move to New York and help that orphanage get their new building! It's the right thing to do. I just feel like it's your father speaking to us from Heaven and guiding us in that direction."

So move they did. And for more than fourteen years now, "Dr. Joe" and "Mrs. Ruth" had been reading books to the children on a daily basis. There had been times, of course, when Joey had been called out of town on business and had therefore not been able to make it to the facility, but "Mrs. Rose" had been there every day for almost a decade and a half.

Not only did she finally have her own set of kids, but she'd been there so long that many of the kids who had moved out of the orphanage as young adults were now bringing their own children to the facility to meet the woman who had helped shape their lives. Rose considered these second-generation kids to be her "grandchildren," so in the end, Joey had fulfilled his promise for delivering her grandchildren after all.

When Mrs. Rose had finally succumbed to cancer last week, the children had all been devastated. Dr. Joe wasn't feeling real happy about it himself, but he knew that he had to put on his best face and help the children all understand about growing old and dying. He had to let them know how happy they had all made his mother, and how all she would ever want is for them to go out into the world and do good things for other people.

On a normal day, Joey would have been coming to the center to read the children passages from one of his favorite classics. He had a special way of turning even the most antiquated storylines into a modernized adventure that would keep the children fascinated for weeks as he worked his way through the prose, chapter by chapter. And for all those years and all those pages, Joey had used the same bookmark: a tattered and creased cardboard lithograph of Frank Bowerman, 1-7/16 inches wide and 2-5/8 inches high. It was a tribute to the father he had never known.

It turns out that Joey had never been able to find a buyer for the hundreds of Bowerman cards that he'd discovered in his father's trunk those many moons ago. He had been able to sell a few of the old newspapers for spare change, but the baseball cards of an unknown player were worthless to everyone, just as his mother had predicted. He had decided to keep them and was glad now that he did because he found himself misplacing his bookmark about every six months or so. At this rate, he still had enough of the Bowerman bookmarks to keep losing them at that rate for another two centuries.

At one time in the late 1960's, Joey had asked one of his contemporaries at Sotheby's to do some research and determine the current market value -- if one even existed -- of his cards. His friend put him in touch with a local baseball card dealer, and as Joey expected, the news was more amusing than anything else.

"Sorry," this nice young man named Barry had told him, "but everyone I know in the hobby would agree that your card is virtually worthless. The card is from a very popular group of tobacco cards known as the T-206 set, but your guy Bowerman is a nobody. Probably worth a dime apiece in mint condition. Now if you had a Honus Wagner from that set, then we'd be talking about something special. A Wagner in good condition would probably fetch something like $250 at a card show."

Joey remembered doing the math in his head, multiplying $250 times the five hundred or so cards that he had back home and nearly fainting when he came up with $125,000. The 1968 Oldsmobile he'd just purchased brand new had only cost him $2,800; he could have bought the whole dealership and the ground it stood on if his dad had only been a fan of Wagner instead of Bowerman!

The memories of that conversation gave Joey a well-needed chuckle as he put his head down and trudged through the blizzard towards the orphanage, his book for the day and his ever-present bookmark gripped tightly in his hands.

Today was going to be a different experience. Today instead of a vintage classic, "Dr. Joe" was going to read a recently published book to the kids; a children's book, in fact. It would never be considered a rare book by any stretch of the imagination, but Joey considered it a sentimental favorite and knew that it would deliver his message of generosity to the children better than he could. He wanted to really leave a mark on the children and be sure that their final mental images of his mother were of her great generosity and charitableness.

Joey made his way through the front doors, shaking the snow from his overcoat and removing his scarf. He knew he would have to try hard not to burst into tears as he read to the children so as not to frighten some of the younger ones, yet he knew that he had never made it through this book without crying. He had resigned himself into knowing that today would be no different.

As he hung his coat in the closet and headed down the hallway to the reading room full of children -- a well-worn copy of *"The Giving Tree"* in his trembling hands -- Joey said a few Hail Mary's for courage. He knew his mother was watching from somewhere up above and would give him the strength to get through this.

Chapter 9

Atlanta
2007

"What!?"

I had to hold the phone away from my ear to keep my eardrum from bursting. My conversation with Jerry Johns was clearly *not* going as planned.

"You just don't get it, do you?" he shouted. "Do you have any idea what it's like to be a world-class athlete?"

I remembered that I had once been one of the best quarters players in all of Gainesville during law school, but I decided that this was probably not the best time to mention it.

The Stickman continued to rant. "Do you know what drives all of us to be the best at what we do? It's ego, man, nothing but pure ego! I don't want the pitcher to embarrass me, and he don't want me to embarrass him. It's all about respect. It's all about being the best. And it's all about *having* the best!

You think a guy like me can drive up in a freakin' Buick, man? Hell naw! Don't let those Tiger Woods ads fool you, Chuck, ain't no way Tiger's driving up to the Jiffy Mart in no Buick while his wife drives the Ferrari up and down Rodeo Drive!"

"Tiger Woods got married?" I said in jest. "Who'd he marry, his old grade school sweetheart? Probably a dumpy little mouse who can cook?"

"Don't play dumb with me, damn it, you know good and well who he married. Like I said, it's all about *having* the best if you want to be considered the best by all the other athletes, so Tiger went and got him pretty damn close to the best. Ha, Buick! I'd like to see him try to make her drive a Buick. She'd get to the restaurant and give the valet the keys and just tell him he could *have* the damn thing!"

I was about to jump in, but apparently the Stickman was on a roll. He was Neidermeyer and I was Flounder, and all I could do was take my beating like a man.

"What makes you think I want a stupid baseball card that's done been bent up and all? I'd be the laughingstock of the clubhouse if I came in there with an old ratty-ass piece of shit like that and said I paid $200,000 for it. Those guys don't know who Honus Wagner is, man.

The only old Pittsburgh Pirate they ever heard of is Roberto Clemente, and that's only 'cause he died while he was still playing. You trying to embarrass me or something, wanting me to buy an old second-rate hand-me-down card like that?"

I tried to explain my logic behind all the reasons why he should settle for one of the other forty-nine T-206 Wagner cards for his investment portfolio, but he would have none of it.

"I thought I made it clear yesterday," he growled, "but what we have here is a failure to communicate. I don't want *any* baseball card; I want *that* baseball card. I want to be the biggest dick in the locker room, the cock of the walk. I want the world to know that the best baseball player in the world owns the best baseball card in the world.

I ain't out here playing to be the forty-fifth best player in the game, and I ain't settling for no forty-fifth place card. Do I need to start making some phone calls to find someone who can get it for me?"

"No, no, I'll get it, I promise," I heard myself pleading.

"That's a good boy, now go fetch!" he screamed as he hung up.

I got on the intercom and buzzed my assistant to see if Alex and Jim were free. When they came in, I gave them the short version of Stickman's answer (not "no," but "hell no") and let them know that we now had one goal and one goal only: to get our hands on that card. I told Jim to call Mr. Stone and see if his client would make a deal.

Hopefully he'd say yes.

"Say You Will" – Foreigner, 1987.

Chapter 10

New York City
June, 2007

At eighty-nine years of age, Dr. Joe Marinolli, Jr. was confined to a motorized wheelchair and had been for several years, but his mental faculties were all still as sharp as ever. He truly believed that he was the oldest living polio survivor in the country, and his research to date had not proven him wrong.

It was amazing what he could get done with the internet; he had probably done more research in the past five years from his wheelchair than he had done in the previous sixty years combined. He was now known worldwide as one of the preeminent scholars on rare works of literature, but he had come to believe that *all* books would be rare once everything was just put on the web instead.

When he had finally given up his independence and moved into an assisted living facility, "Dr. Joe" had specifically chosen one that was in close proximity to his kids. He credited his daily interaction with the children at the orphanage for keeping him feeling young at heart, and he had already made the legal preparations to have his now sizeable estate left to the orphanage at his death. He knew that the $500,000 or so that he had stored away in tax-free bonds would only be a drop in the bucket comparatively speaking -- given how large the New York Foundling had grown – but to him the act was more about the sacrifice than it was about the amount itself.

Just like his mother had given a large portion of her life to the children, Joe (he hadn't been called "Joey" by anyone since she had passed thirty-seven years earlier) knew that there were literally thousands of individuals whose lives had been affected by his volunteer work. He took pride in this, and he only wished that he could do more before his time on earth drew to a close.

One particular area of concern for Joe was the recent bad news that he had learned from the organization's Chief Financial Officer, Tom Bennett, as the two of them were having coffee in the cafeteria last week.

"I don't know how to break it to the kids, Joe," Tom had said wistfully as he sipped from his oversized mug, "but I think we're going to lose Stratton Park."

Joe nearly fell out of his wheelchair! Stratton Park was one of the only remaining undeveloped plots in reasonable proximity to the orphanage; more importantly, it was the only place where the kids could get outside to play and get any kind of recreation. The park had a playground, basketball courts and even a baseball field where the orphanage youth baseball league held their games. If this wonderful park was turned into another high-rise building, there was simply nowhere else for the children to turn.

Joe had even become a bit of a baseball fan in recent years, ever since some of his children had asked him to come watch their games. There were a total of eight different teams in the orphanage's "league," and every team consisted of both boys and girls from ages twelve to sixteen. The games were very competitive, and several chores around the orphanage were performed by the individuals who came out on the losing end of the previous night's games.

One game in particular still stood our in Joe's mind as symbolic of what the park meant to the children. There was one young boy in the orphanage of mixed-race heritage named Roland, and Roland was born with birth defects that caused his arms not to develop fully. Joe suspected that it was because his mother had been a drug abuser, but unfortunately that was the case with a lot of the kids here. Joe and Roland shared a particularly strong bond since Joe had battled polio as a child, so Roland would always seek comfort and reassurance from "Dr. Joe" whenever someone would call him "Lobster Boy" or "Alligator Arms."

Naturally, Roland was never selected to play in any of the pick up games that arose at Stratton Park, but he had accepted his fate and would still walk to the park every day with hopes of being picked. Inevitably, he would end up watching from the stands with a sad look of dejection on his face.

One night, Joe had spoken to one of the counselors about having Roland appointed as the official batboy for all of the baseball games. At first it was a slight struggle for Roland to pick the bats up off the ground with his handicap, but he finally got to where he could kneel down and scoop them up with ease. He loved his newfound involvement with the games, and he took to his task with fervor. He made sure the aluminum bats were scrubbed and shiny before putting them away after the games, and he memorized which kids liked to use which bats.

Roland was quick on his feet, so his involvement really did help speed up the games and make things flow a lot smoother for everyone. And best of all for Roland, since he was the batboy for both teams, he never actually lost a game. This meant that he was excused from ever having to do any of the tougher chores back at the orphanage. But where other kids would have gloated at this and rubbed it in by sitting back and relaxing while everyone else worked, Roland never did. He *wanted* to fit in, so he always tried to pitch in wherever he could.

One night last month, an especially important game was shaping up at Stratton Park. This was like an annual All-Star game of sorts, because the losing side in this one, and their followers, had to eat baked beans and franks for dinner, while the winners and their fans ate big juicy steaks. Not that the beans and franks were much different than what the kids ate every night, but the steaks were donated by a local meat market and many times it was the *only* steak these kids had ever tasted.

The teams had been chosen at a large gathering where the entire orphanage was present, and then all of the other kids were assigned a team for which to cheer. Needless to say, this game was a colossal event for everyone.

As the game wore on, it was obvious that neither side held a distinct advantage. Finally, with the game tied in the bottom half of the last inning, the "National League" team got a runner on first by laying down a bunt. It was a bang-bang play at first, but the runner lunged for the bag and barely beat out the throw from third.

Unfortunately, the runner had stepped on the corner of the bag when making his stretch and rolled his ankle. It swelled up like a melon almost immediately, and he was carried off the field so that the counselors could put some ice on his injury.

This left the Nationals with a big dilemma, since the go ahead run was now on first base. They needed a pinch runner who could really move, but the only two available players on the bench were big overweight boys who were picked solely on their ability to mash the ball. Neither of them would ever score from first unless they were carted around the bases in a wheelbarrow.

Suddenly, Joe had an inspiration, and he drove his wheelchair over to the fenced backstop to speak with the counselor who was coaching the Nationals. "Hey, Mike, can I make a suggestion?"

Mike jogged over to the backstop. "Sure, Dr. Joe, but if you're thinking about calling it a tie game so that everyone leaves a winner, it's not an option. They're already cooking the steaks back home, so there's only going to be enough for half of the kids. If we end the game now and call it a tie, it will be a zoo back there."

"No, that wasn't what I was thinking," Joe said. "What about putting Roland in to run? You know he's faster than those two on your bench, and what's the worst thing that could happen?"

Mark thought about it. "The worst thing that could happen is that he could start running the bases the wrong way. I'm not sure he would even know what to do out there."

"If you and I talk to him for a second and make sure he understands the rules, will you give it a shot? I know it would mean the world to him, and it won't matter anyway unless your team gets another hit. You're one away from extra innings, so after he runs, you can substitute one of the other kids to play in the field if the game continues."

Mark nodded his head and turned to the bench. "Roland, come over here a sec!" he shouted.

Roland had been busy getting the bat ready for the next Nationals hitter, so he was caught by surprise. He hustled over to the fence. "Yeah coach?"

"Roland, you've been out here for years watching these games, so you know how it works to run the bases right?" Joe asked.

Roland nodded eagerly, but his eyes looked like a deer frozen in the headlights of an oncoming semi.

"If we put you in to run," Mark said, "you know that you go from first to second to third to home, right?"

Roland nodded again, nervously swaying from side to side as he stood at the fence.

"Roland," Joe said, looking him straight in the eyes, "you know that I had polio as a child and never got a chance to ever play baseball. So you're not just going out there for yourself, your going out there for me too, okay?"

Roland continued nodding, and in fact had been nodding his head continuously throughout the whole conversation. He looked like a bobble head doll in the dashboard of 1975 Chevy Nova traveling down a bumpy dirt road.

"Okay Roland, put on a helmet and get out there," Mark said, "and just run as fast as you can."

Roland just stood there nodding like he'd been hypnotized.

"Um, *now* Roland," Mark said again.

Finally Roland snapped out if it and went to find a helmet. He cradled one in his underdeveloped arms and lowered his head down into it. He trotted out to first base, looking something very close to the Great Gazoo from *Flinstones* fame.

The crowd all cheered and yelled his name as he stood out there. Even fans for the American League squad were elated to see "Ro" finally get his chance to participate. A chant of "Let's Go, Ro!" broke out from the bleachers.

Unfortunately, as Joe had predicted, the next two pitches were strikes, so the inning was one strike away from being over. Roland would be replaced for defensive purposes, so it looked as if he would go down in history as having a shorter career than Moonlight Graham.

With no balls and two strikes, the pitcher for the Americans tried to strike the batter out with a curveball in the dirt. The batter refused to swing at the bad pitch, and it bounced past the catcher to the backstop. Roland didn't move.

"Go, Roland, go!" shouted Mark from the bench, and Roland shot off like a cannon. He accelerated like there was no tomorrow and he reached second base just as the catcher was picking up the ball and turning around to toss it back to the pitcher. But to everyone's surprise, Roland kept running as fast as he could around second and started heading to third! He had no idea what he was doing, but he had heard Mark yell "Go" and he was going to go, go, go!

The catcher was caught by surprise, but still had plenty of time to throw Roland out at third. Joe's heart sank to his stomach; now Roland was actually going to *cost* his team a chance at winning the game. He wouldn't even know how to get into a pickle or how to slide if necessary. But one thing Roland *did* know how to do is run fast, so that he did.

Fortunately for Roland's team, the catcher wasn't the only one caught by surprise. The third baseman had been watching things unfold and had not gone over to cover third base. When he finally realized that Roland was coming his way, he sprinted over to the bag, but it was too late to give his catcher a stationary target. The catcher was momentarily distracted, and his throw sailed slightly wide into foul territory. The third baseman lunged and was able to get a glove on it, but he couldn't hang on to it and it trickled a few feet away. Good Lord, Roland was actually going to be safe at third with the go ahead run!

Unless, of course, the unthinkable happened – which it did. Roland, by now hitting on all cylinders, was in his *Chariots of Fire* moment. He couldn't see or hear anything around him, and his tiny little arms were pumping up and down like finely tuned pistons. Joe thought to himself that Roland looked like a Tyrannosaurus Rex chasing down its next meal.

Just like there was no turning back the Millennium Falcon once Chewy had kicked it into hyperspace, there was no stopping Ro at this point. All he knew was that he wanted to score for Dr. Joe, so he hit third base at warp speed and sprinted for home!

By now, everyone was on his or her feet screaming for one thing or another. One part of the crowd was yelling for Ro to score, one part was shouting for the third baseman to throw him out at home, and the younger kids who didn't even understand the game were just screaming because everyone else was screaming.

By the time the third baseman had run over to grab the ball, Roland was halfway home. But the third baseman had a rifle for an arm, so he uncorked a laser beam toward the plate where the catcher stood waiting for the throw. Joe had nearly swallowed his tongue by this time, and despite all the ruckus, all he could hear in his head was Yankee broadcaster Phil Rizzuto's one contribution to rock and roll:

"Paradise By the Dashboard Lights" – Meatloaf, 1977

Here comes the throw, here comes Ro; there's going to be a play at the plate. Holy Cow, I think Ro's gonna make it!
Thoonk!

The throw had hit Roland square in the helmet, sounding like a melon being dropped on the supermarket floor. The ball bounced away and Roland fell forward like a bad actor being shot in a Western -- except that Roland's arms couldn't brace his fall, so he skidded and bounced down the base path like a water skier who had fallen but refused to let go of the tow rope.

Mercifully Roland's body finally came to stop just inches from the plate and he lay there motionless in the dirt. Meanwhile, the catcher had gone over to gather up the baseball and was sprinting back to tag Roland out. The umpire was crouched over the scene, ready to make the call.

As the catcher was starting his dive towards Roland's legs to tag him out, a miracle happened. Roland's body spasmed once, and then as if being pulled on string from above, one of Roland's little flipper arms swung up from underneath his body and reached out as far as it could, barely grazing the edge of home plate just as the catcher landed on his backside.

"Safe!" yelled the umpire, swinging his arms wide to give the signal.

A tumultuous roar erupted from the stands and everyone swarmed onto the field. By this time, Roland had shaken off the cobwebs and raised himself into a sitting position, just before being hoisted up by the larger kids and thrust upon their shoulders in celebration. Joe couldn't get his wheelchair onto the field, but he was right there by the fence cheering and clapping as loud as anyone; tears of joy and amazement streaming down his face.

Joe knew that he had lived a full life, but this moment would stick with him as the most thrilling and moving event of which he had ever been a part. He had never attended a major league game, but he knew it would pale in comparison to the joy he had seen in the eyes of those kids. Like everyone else, Joe knew what the average salary was for a big league ballplayer, so he couldn't imagine those overpaid prima donnas hugging each other and celebrating with the same emotion as those kids.

"Roland's Mad Dash" would be remembered for posterity by anyone who had witnessed it, and it was the main reason why Joe was so crestfallen at the news Tom Bennett had delivered.

"But I thought the orphanage owned Stratton Park outright?" Joe replied with a look of confusion on his face. "I thought the Stratton family donated it to the orphanage back in the seventies when they were setting up their foundation?"

Tom nodded and then began rubbing his temples, looking like a man with the weight of the world on his back. "That's true, but do you have any idea how much that land is worth? Five acres in downtown Manhattan? We're talking beaucoup bucks, easily twenty million or so; probably a lot more. We started borrowing against the land about fifteen years ago to help fund various building projects and whatnot, and now with interest rates rising again, the monthly payments on the mortgage are killing us.

We're already five months behind on the payments, and the huge balloon payment comes due at the end of this month. The Board of Directors has voted against borrowing more money to pay off the balloon because we would have to put up this building as collateral, so the bank's going to have no choice but to foreclose. Of course, I'm convinced that the bank wants to own the land themselves as the site for their new world headquarters, so the last thing they care about is whether a few orphans have a place to play baseball."

"How much are we talking in all?" Joe had asked, thinking about his nest egg.

"Seven million," Tom replied with a dejected look on his face. "There's no way we can raise it this quick, and we've already exhausted all of our normal philanthropic efforts."

Tom got up from the table, dumping the rest of his untouched coffee in the sink. "I'm too depressed to eat or drink," he said. "How are we going to tell the kids, Joe? How are we going to tell them that their favorite pastime is no more?"

A week had passed since that conversation between Tom and Joe, but still nobody had told the children anything. It was as if everyone was praying for a miracle that they knew would never come. Joe had racked his brain every night trying to think of different ways to come up with the money, but it was just too big of a hurdle to overcome. He sighed in desperation and began logging on to his laptop to check out the latest news on CNN.com. One of the headlines caught his eye: *Rare Toy Collection Sold for Record Price.*

Joe clicked on the story out of sheer curiosity and couldn't believe that someone would pay $1,580,000 for a bunch of old Lionel trains and mechanical banks? What had the world come to? Why couldn't that person have donated his money to a charity instead? All it would take is a few contributions like this and the kids would get to keep Stratton Park.

Wait a minute! Lionel trains and mechanical banks? A jolt of excitement shot through Joe's body, followed immediately by a wave of panic. He had a whole trunk full of those same antique toys – the ones he had put in his father's old footlocker some half-century ago in pristine condition – but what the heck had he done with that trunk? Where had it gone when they had moved him into the assisted living facility?

Joe still had powerful connections at Sotheby's, so he knew that he could use those contacts to find a quick buyer for his treasure trove of toys. Add that to his nest egg, and now he might be able to come up with a good chunk of what it would take to save the park. It certainly wouldn't satisfy the whole mortgage, but it would be enough to borrow against in order to buy some more time and let the orphanage try more fundraising.

Heck, if he could publicize the cause, it would raise the stakes for his toy auction because high rollers always spend more when the money is going to charity and not to one of their peers. It was just human nature – especially with the ego-driven "Type A" collectors who could drop a hundred thousand dollars at the blink of an eye just to have the finest or rarest example of anything.

He just *had* to find that chest. Had he left it in his attic when they'd moved him here?

"Toys In the Attic" – Aerosmith, 1975.

Chapter 11

Atlanta
2007

Barry Stone was being very tightlipped with me over the phone, but I could tell from his queries and suggestions that a deal could be made if the price was right.

"You know, Mr. Stone, your client isn't the only person in the world with a T-206 Wagner, but he could be the only one to have box seat tickets to a game of his choice, admission to the locker room and a professional photo session with The Big Stick and his teammates.

But on top of that, he'd be able to take with him Jerry John's entire outfit from the game -- from hat to cleats to jersey to glove to chewed bubble gum – and the Stick will autograph every single item right there in front of a licensed authenticator. Your client will get a photograph of the Stick signing each item and handing it to your client, so along with the certificates of authenticity, every one of those items will be worth their weight in gold. Their pedigree will be one-of-a-kind."

I could sense that Stone was calculating the market values in his head of each item, so I sweetened the pot just a tad. "We'll throw in some cash as well to make up the small difference in value, and of course we'll reward you for your help in all of this by allowing you into the clubhouse as well. You can bring in whatever items you want signed by Jerry Johns and I'm sure you'll be able to get a few photos as well."

At this point, I expected Stone to be eating out of my hand, practically begging me to close the deal. His reply shocked me back into reality.

"Mr. Evans, I must admit that your offer is a generous one, and that if handled properly as an in-kind trade, it is one that would have great tax benefits to both sides. But I'm afraid I have some bad news for you. Two other potential buyers have made inquiries about purchasing the card, and I owe it to my client to get the best deal possible for him."

My heart sank. Or was this just more negotiation tactics on his part? "How do I know you aren't just making this up for purposes of leverage over me, Mr. Stone?"

"First of all," he replied, "you need to remember that *you* called *me*, Mr. Evans, not the other way around. One of us has something that the other one wants, and we both know it. If your client can't afford to pay the price, then he needs to seek Pete's advice in *O Brother Where Art Thou:* do *not* seek the treasure.

The price of the artifact is steep, but with the recent sale of the card making national news, the interest in these Wagner cards is extremely heavy right now. I don't need to lie to you for leverage purposes; I've already got all the leverage I need."

"Point taken," I admitted, "but you also have to admit that the $2,500,000 price tag was set at a public auction, where everyone on the planet could bid as high as they wanted to bid. Thus, you can't deny that there was *nobody on earth* who was willing to bid more than $2,500,000 for the card last week. Can you see where I would be dubious of other potential buyers suddenly popping up out of the woodwork?"

"Certainly," he replied. "So where does that leave us?"

I thought for a moment. "Can you tell me the names of the interested parties?"

"One of them has asked to remain confidential, so I can't disclose his name," Stone said, "but I presume you've heard of Duke University?"

"Of course I have, but what the heck do they have to do with this?"

"Well, for starters they have a billion dollar endowment fund that their trustees manage, so they have plenty of cash to buy whatever they want."

"Okay," I said, still trying to put the pieces together.

"And second, are you forgetting who the true original owner of the T-206 Honus Wagner card was?"

"I thought that nobody owned any because they weren't supposed to exist?" I said.

"Precisely. But who was it that had them printed for their financial gain?"

Then it hit me. "The American Tobacco Company. Which was owned by James B. Duke."

"Exactamundo."

"So Duke University wants to buy it back as an investment and display it on campus somewhere as part of a tribute to the Duke family legacy?"

"That's what they're saying publicly," Stone said in a lower voice. "But between me and you, I think the recent news of the worth of this card has some of them a little scared."

"About what?"

"At his death, James Duke left a large portion of his estate to the University. You're a lawyer; if you have a case against a defendant and he dies, who do you sue in his place?"

"His estate."

"Bingo. And if you have a good case but your plaintiff dies before you can file suit, who can bring the case on behalf of the deceased?"

"*His* estate."

"You got it. So...if I were a descendant of Honus Wagner and I was sitting around one morning in my small apartment drinking instant coffee and getting ready to go work a twelve-hour shift at the factory...and I found out that my ancestor's image had been duplicated without his permission and was now worth a gazillion dollars...I don't think I'd have any problems finding a hungry lawyer to sue James Dukes' estate for using his unlicensed image."

I have to admit, the wheels of opportunity were spinning in my head as he was laying it all out.

"So if the Wagner family won in court, wouldn't *they* then own the card?" I said as I was thinking out loud. "Wouldn't that actually come back to hurt *your* client, since he might have to part with the card?"

"No, it wasn't improper under the New York Privacy Act of 1903 for the tobacco company to print the cards, just like it wouldn't have been illegal for a child to draw colored pictures of Honus Wagner. What *was* illegal, however, was using the photos *for monetary gain.*

Therefore, since these Wagner cards are floating out in public, the legal presumption would be that they were actually inserted into cigarette packs and distributed to the public. So not only could a lawsuit be brought for the value of the card itself, but also for a portion of the profits that the cigarette company made during the three years that the cards were being inserted in the packs. Given the huge profits that the American Tobacco Company made between 1909 and 1911 – remember it was so profitable that the Supreme Court had to use the anti-trust laws to break it up -- and the inflation that has occurred since that time, I'm guessing that $2,500,000 is chump change compared to what we're talking about."

"Man oh man," I said in bewilderment. "No wonder they want to get the card back. They may not want to display it, they may want to destroy it!"

"That's what I'm thinking," said Stone. "I've done some research, and it looks to me like the last eleven private sales of T-206 Wagner cards were to someone representing the Duke University Foundation. I don't have any way of knowing whether or not they destroyed those cards, but I sure haven't seen them putting them on a road tour."

"So why didn't they buy this one at the auction last week?"

Stone chuckled. "Just a stroke of luck on our part. Literally. From what I hear, a stroke of lightening hit the office building where they were all standing around the computer placing their last-second bids over the internet. I was at the auction in person, and I had no idea who I was bidding against over the internet. I was expecting them to bid again since they had shown no signs of hesitation at all, but suddenly no more bids came and the hammer struck down with me the winner."

"So if I'm reading you right," I stated, "you want to have your client sell his card to Duke's Foundation as soon as possible before it gets tied up or confiscated in any sort of copyright or trademark litigation? Don't rock the boat, huh?"

"Yep, you've got the notion. Hues Corporation, by the way. 1974. Great song. But sure, we want to flip the card quick, and if we can make a profit doing it, even better. There's no way I can advise my client to turn down what Duke's offering him with everything I now know about the card.

And even though I don't represent your side of this transaction, I'm far too honest to sell you the card with the knowledge of this information; that'd be a serious breach of ethics on my part. I think the only people I can sell it to now in good faith are the folks at Duke, so I'm afraid it's '*no soup for you.*' I know this isn't what you wanted to hear, Mr. Evans, but hopefully I've saved you and your client a great deal of hassle and heartache."

After hearing everything that Stone had to say, I felt a whole lot better about letting the card go elsewhere. I knew Jerry Johns would sue us in a heartbeat if we spent his money on the card and then lost it in litigation, so I would draft up a full legal memorandum explaining our position for him so that he could see how we had actually saved him from making a terrible move.

"Thanks, Mr. Stone, I think I owe you one. I'll let you know the next time Jerry's got a game in New York and we'll leave you some tickets and dugout passes. I doubt he'll sign anything for you, but it's the least I can do."

As we hung up, I started thinking about how crazy this whole thing was and whether or not the people at Duke would ever be able to purchase all of the remaining Wagner cards. I barely passed Economics 101 in college, but it seemed to me like these remaining cards were only going to get more and more valuable as the supply started dwindling. If only I could get my hands on some of these cards.

I made a note to talk to Alex and Jim about pooling our savings and maybe doing just that. Or maybe even the firm's 401(k) fund? Why not – it takes money to make money, right?

"Money" – Pink Floyd, 1973.

Chapter 12

New York City
July, 2007

Joe Marinolli knew that his old heart was on its last leg, and it couldn't take much more. In the past three weeks, Joe had been through a roller coaster ride of emotions that had taken its toll on him both physically and mentally. The thrill of victory and the agony of defeat had come so close together that they had shaken him hard.

The good news had come first; Joe had finally located his father's old trunk. One of the movers specifically remembered loading that old trunk on the moving truck and hauling it away from Joe's house when Joe had moved into the assisted living facility.

"Yeah, I remember that old thing because it was so heavy," the mover had told Joe over the phone when Joe had finally located him.

"Well where'd you put it?" Joe asked frantically.

"I delivered it just like it was marked," the mover replied. "It said right on the side '*Property of New York Foundling,*' so that's where I took it. Dropped it off right at the front door. Had 'em sign for it and everything. I'm sure the moving company still has the receipt if you don't believe me."

Upon hearing this, Joey had raced over to the orphanage as fast as his motorized wheelchair could take him. He'd searched high and low for someone who remembered the trunk being delivered, and had finally found someone who had been here during that time.

"Sure, I remember when that trunk came. Nobody knew where it had come from, but we get anonymous contributions and donations all the time, so nobody thought anything of it," Tameka Messing, one of the senior nurses on the children's wing had said to Joe. "Wasn't nothing in there but a bunch of really old trains and stuff. Kids these days don't play with anything that isn't on a computer or doesn't have a computer in it, so best I can remember, after a while they just took the trunk and whatever was left in it down to the basement. That's the last I've seen of it, and that was a while ago."

That sent Joe wheeling down to the basement, where he enlisted the services of Pete Coughlin, the head of maintenance, to help him search for the trunk. After searching for hours and moving hundreds of items from one side of the basement to the other, Pete and his crew were ready to quit.

"Tell me again what this treasure is that we're supposed to be hunting," Pete had asked with a tone of serious doubt in his voice. Joe could tell that Pete thought he was just another 89-year old man who couldn't remember what he had eaten for breakfast that morning, so he went out of his way to make sure Pete knew that he was on the ball.

"It's a very old trunk that I'll recognize as soon as I see it, and I can't recall the specifics about everything that was once inside it, but one thing I remember for sure was my old Ive's Railway Circus Train Set. From what I could find on the internet, the last one sold at auction in Philadelphia in 2003 for more than seventy thousand dollars – and it was in nowhere near the condition that mine was in," Joe stated firmly. "That's just a tiny bit of what was in that trunk, so at least you can see that I'm not making you do all this work for nothing. I'm just trying to find the stuff so that I can sell it and donate the proceeds to the orphanage."

Joe's message was received loud and clear, and the work crew went back to the search with renewed effort. Just ten minutes later, euphoria had set in when the trunk had been spotted sitting underneath an old foosball table that had become useless when all of the men had come off of the poles.

"It sure is heavy, Mr. Pete," one of the workers said as they slid the trunk out into an open area. I think this thing is still loaded with trains."

Joe had wheeled himself over as close as he could get and waited with baited breath while Pete reached over and popped open the lid.

Everyone just stared in hushed amazement.

Finally one of Pete's crew broke the silence.

"Did you say 'trains' or 'drains,' mister?" he snickered, bringing muffled laughter from everyone except Joe.

Inside the trunk was an old porcelain sink, faucets and all. No sign of any trains or toys at all. Just the sink, resting on a musty old felt blanket.

"I've heard of people taking everything but the kitchen sink," Pete said, "but I've never actually seen it with my own eyes. I remember when we removed that sink from the break room a few years ago, but how it ended up in that trunk I have no clue."

Joe could only sit in his wheelchair and stare at the empty trunk. Hs eyes filled with tears, and he had come so close to helping the orphanage save Stratton Park.

"I guess it's still your trunk, Dr. Joe," Pete said compassionately. "Do you want me to have one of the guys carry it back to your residence with you?"

Joe had no real need for the trunk, but he did have a large collection of books that he could store in it. But more importantly, it was a link to his dad, the father he had never known.

"Yes, I think I would like that very much. Thank you," Joe replied.

Later that evening, back in his room at the facility, Joe began gathering up his books to put them in the chest. When he opened it up, he realized just how musty the old blanket had become. I'll just take that out and have them wash it or donate it to the orphanage if it's even salvageable.

As he removed the folded blanket from the bottom of the chest, he noticed a large artist's sketch pad that had been underneath the blanket at the bottom of the trunk for what appeared to be a very long time.

"*American Lithograph Company, New York, New York, 1909,*" he read to himself from the cover of the pad. He began to flip through the pages, but realized pretty quickly that the pad was brand new and had never been used. None of the pages had been drawn on and none appeared to have been torn out. He wondered how the pad had found its way into the trunk, and he found himself wishing very much that his father had left him a note inside the pages.

He knew in his heart that his father had only been fifteen years old in 1909, but he hoped that maybe his father had pulled the pad out of the trunk at some later date and drawn a sketch or a note to the wife and young child that he was about to leave behind as he headed off to war.

Just as he reached the last blank page and felt his tears start to come again, 89-year-old Joey Marinolli Jr. finally found his father's buried treasure. There it was, wedged between the last sheet of paper and the cardboard back cover of the pad, stored for safekeeping. It was the last full sheet of cards from the Bowerman heist -- thirty cards in all -- in gem mint condition.

Chapter 13

Atlanta
2007

When we were finished laying it all out for the Big Stick, he was extremely disappointed but somewhat understanding of the situation. By the time Monday morning rolled around, things at work had settled back to normal pace, and my dad still had fifteen days left to shoot whatever it was he was hunting in Africa.

"Maybe he's hunting spider monkeys," Jim said. *"I'm gonna come at you like a spider monkey, Chuck!"*

I had to laugh at a black guy trying to do a redneck accent. "The guy in the movie was named Ricky Bobby, not Reggie Roby," I reminded him.

"Well," Jim stated with a sly grin, "that was *Talladega Nights*, and my version is *Tellanegro Nights*. That's just one of the benefits of being black; I have more access to certain jokes than you do. It's kind of like reparations for black comedians and musicians. You know, affirmative action and all that." Jim flashed me a big Al Jolson smile.

"Hey, maybe my dad will shoot a gorilla," I said, "only to find out later that is was Clarence Beeks! *It - was - the - Dukes! It - was - the - Dukes!*"

"Man, *Trading Places*; what a classic! That was back when Dan Akroyd was still funny," Jim said. "Speaking of Duke and millionaires, did you ever confirm with Barry Stone whether or not they closed the deal on that card?"

"Yep, they sure did," I answered. "He wasn't allowed to tell me the price, but he said that his client was just happy to be done with it and that he could now afford to buy a whole bunch of regular Honus Wagner cards with the profit."

Jim shook his head in amazement. "I just can't believe that a piece of cardboard with a funny picture of a man with a big nose is worth *that* much money."

"*Hello-o-o, McFly-y-y?*" I said, leaning over to rap him on the side of the head. "Have you ever seen the old master paintings that sell for tens of millions of dollars each? They're nothing but a bunch of ugly fat naked girls with some nymphs or babies in the background. It's not about the art, like the Stickman said, it's about the bragging rights that come with owning one."

"I guess you're right," Jim agreed, "but if I had pictures of a naked lady *that* ugly, I sure wouldn't hang 'em up on the wall. I guess Sir Mixalot would have been in heaven back in those old days, huh?"

"Hey, no fair pulling the race card and going rap on me," I said jokingly. "What song did he do?

Jim laughed. "I should have known a bow-tie wearing cracker like yourself wouldn't know. Sir Mixalot did *I Like Big Butts.*"

"Oh yeah, I've heard that one," I admitted. "I just had no clue who sang it. I guess Mixalot and Freddy Mercury were in the same camp, since Queen sang that song *Fat Bottomed Girls.*"

"Damn," Jim said, "the dude was gay and liked fat bottomed girls, but he was a hell of a rocker. That must have been some scene backstage -- one bunch of skinny male groupies and another bunch of big-assed female groupies! Be like a freak show at the circus back there!"

Jim and I continued our deep philosophical conversation for another few minutes until Alex walked in the room with a glum expression and stooped shoulders.

"Why the long face, Secretariat?" I asked.

"I know," Jim blurted out, "*Blue Morning, Blue Day*, by Foreigner, right?"

"You're more right than you'll ever know, my brother from another mother," Alex said, trying to lift his own spirits. "It's a blue day all right – Duke Blue Devils blue."

Jim and I looked at each other, perplexed by what Alex meant.

"What happened, did Coach K finally quit," I asked, knowing that Alex was a Dookie through and through. "Or did the clock finally strike twelve, turning him back into Gus the rat?"

"No," Alex said, "it's a lot more serious than that. I got a call today from the dean of the law school. Apparently they found out that I worked here, and they know somehow that our firm was trying to buy that Honus Wagner card."

"Yeah," I stated, "I told Stone that he could use our name to help try and sweeten any deal he could make with the

University. I told him he could identify us as a potential buyer so that it might give him leverage. I didn't see any harm in it since we really were potential customers at one time."

"Well, apparently somebody at Duke does, because he let it be known that they might have to re-open that old code of conduct bullshit investigation again if I don't persuade you guys to buzz off on the hunt for any future T-206 Wagner cards. Apparently they didn't appreciate us being involved and driving up the price, and I think they're scared that they may run into us again in future auctions for the rest of the Wagner cards."

"That's a bunch of crap!" I exclaimed. "They exonerated you of those fabricated charges years ago, didn't they? Didn't they finally agree that the other guy was copying off of your paper and not the other way around?"

"Well, yeah, they dropped the issue due to lack of proof and it being my word against his. Plus, I had a 3.95 grade point average at the time and his was in the John Blutarsky range, so I think they knew full well that I wasn't copying off of him."

"So what's the big deal now?" Jim asked.

"Apparently they're hinting that a new witness may have come forward -- anonymously, of course – and decided to come clean about the whole thing. I could fight them on it and still probably win, but just opening the whole dirty mess up again would put a huge red flag on my transcript. I'd never find work anywhere else."

"What a crock," I said, surprised at how serious this whole situation had become. Apparently Duke University was more worried about gathering up all of these baseball cards than I had suspected. "Screw 'em, Alex, you don't need to worry about finding a job anywhere else. You can work here forever."

"Thanks," Alex muttered, "but I'll feel better if you can get that in writing from your dad. I love you and all, but last I checked, he's got a little bit more pull around here than you."

"I told you I would get with him and let him know how much you and Jim had helped us get through this crisis with Jerry Johns, didn't I? You guys are both eligible to make junior partner at the end of the year, so how about if I promise to sit down with my dad and lobby as hard as I can for you guys to get the two available spots over the other thirteen eligible associates?"

Jim sat up to attention at these words. "Alex, my man, don't leave me hanging. Tell the Dookies that they taught you better than that in your ethics classes; that you represent a client and that your duty is *only* to that client and no one else. Except, of course, to *me*, your homeboy! I'm begging you, like Jake Blues would: 'We *need* this gig.' "

"We're on a mission from God," I added, bringing Elwood to the party as well.

Alex stood up straight and got a determined look on his face. "You're right; screw 'em! I owe more to this firm and you guys than I do to those backstabbers, so let's go get ourselves some baseball cards!"

I stood up and walked around the corner of my desk to give Alex a high five. Jim did me one better and gave Alex the big man-hug that can only be pulled out of the closet in truly special occasions. "I knew you'd come through, Alex," Jim shouted. "You're my boy, Blue!"

Chapter 14

New York City
July, 2007

Joe Marinolli stared at the cardboard sheet of uncut baseball cards that he held in his hands. Five different players across the top row, and then the same pattern repeated five more times on the rows below. As he was wondering what the significance of this item was to his father, he noticed that the player pictured in the middle column was none other than Frank Bowerman, so his riddle was solved.

This was how his father had come into possession of all those Frank Bowerman cards! He must have started with a bunch of these sheets and stopped cutting once he got to the last one, deciding to save it unharmed. But how did he get all the sheets in the first place?

Joe turned the sheet over and noticed that sure enough, the backs of the thirty cards were identical to the "*Piedmont Cigarettes*" backs that were on all the Frank Bowerman cards that he had been using as bookmarks for the past few decades.

As he was placing the sheet back into the sketch pad to protect it from getting damaged, another small piece of paper fell out of the pad and fluttered to the floor. Joe leaned over from his wheelchair and picked it up to see what it was.

It was pay stub of some sort, from the American Lithograph Company, dated September 27, 1909, and it indicated that "Marinolli, J." had received "$3.30" for "Week's wages: 10 hours." Joe had never heard his mother mention anything about his dad having worked at the American Lithograph Company, but then he realized that the date of the pay stub would have been from when his father was living at the orphanage. This must have been one of the jobs he'd taken after dropping out of school to support himself.

Joe put the pay stub and the uncut sheet of cards back into the pad and placed it on top of his dresser. He was exhausted after experiencing the euphoria of finding his long-lost trunk and the depression that followed when his now-priceless toy train collection was gone. As he drifted off to sleep, he kept repeating five names in his head; the names of the five players pictured on his father's old sheet of cards.

Brown. Wagner. Bowerman. Young. Kling.

Who were these guys? he thought to himself. Had any of them become famous, or were they just a bunch of old players that time forgot? Why did one of them sound familiar to him. There was a tingling feeling in his brain telling him that something he had heard in the past was trying to force its way back into his memory, but at his age this was becoming a common event. He finally told himself that he would do some research on the card tomorrow – assuming he survived the night – and fell into a deep sleep.

Chapter 15

Atlanta
2007

As was our custom, Alex, Jim and I found ourselves eating lunch at our favorite sports bar so that he could watch ESPN Classic on television while also ogling at the attractive waitresses in their Mitchell & Ness throwback jerseys. One waitress in particular caught my eye. She was wearing an old Kansas City Monarchs jersey and was extremely cute.

Okay, I know -- *baby ducks are cute*. I had to be sure and remind myself not to ever use that word when trying to be romantic with a member of the opposite sex. See, Malenglish users *can* learn something important from watching *Bull Durham*!

As the three of us were sitting on our stools around the high top table, a great tune came on the jukebox. Jim started to sing along quietly about having a dream that had turned to dust and a thought of love that must have been lust.

Then Alex chimed in, raising the volume just a bit, and singing about playing a hand and looking for a joker.

How could I resist joining in for one of the greatest lyrical lines ever? I came in with guns a-blaring, causing us to be now loud enough that we were attracting stares and laughs from other tables.

So now all three of us are belting out the tune, talking about how fate awoke lady luck and now she was waiting outside the door.

I was feeling it now.

I was in the zone.

I was Jordan hitting for sixty-three against the Celtics in the 1986 playoffs; I was DiMaggio in the midst of his streak; I was *en fuego*. I hit the chorus loud and proud, like I was up on stage live at Budokan (wherever the hell that is):

"I'm Win-ning...I'm Win-ning..."

What the hell?

Where were my backup vocals?

I opened my eyes to see Alex and Jim staring at me wide-eyed, neither of them uttering a peep. The sad sacks had hung me out to dry! Then Jim cut his eyes nervously to the area directly behind me and tilted his head in that direction.

Just like the song had said, I turned around there she was: Lady Luck herself. The waitress I had been eyeing was standing right behind me, waiting to take our order.

"So what are you winning?" she asked with a devilish grin on her face. "Surely not a spot on *American Idol* with that rendition."

"As a matter of fact, Simon said that I had unlimited raw potential and Randy called me his 'dawg'," I said smartly. "And please, don't call me Shirley. The name's Chuck."

"Nice to meet you, Chuck, I'm Kristi. Have you ever been to a Turkish prison or watch gladiator movies?"

If three guys' jaws can drop in precise synchronization, ours did. What the heck was this? An attractive female wearing a sports jersey who could recite lines from *Airplane!* as rapidly as Alex could? Had she been cross-trained as a Malenglish spy in her youth?

"I've Been Waiting For a Girl Like You" - Foreigner, 1981.

Okay, that was weird. I hadn't thought of that song since my skating rink days, when all of the other kids were couple skating to it while I played foosball. Why the hell is my brain going all mushy on me now -- right when I need it to come up with a clever Malenglish response? Instead, I just froze like Ralphie in Santa's lap.

"Sorry about the noise," Alex offered, stepping into the void. "We just get caught up in the fever whenever we start singing REO Speedwagon stuff. You should hear us do *Keep On Loving You.* It's magical."

"Yeah," Jim added, "we're thinking about forming an REO Speedwagon cover band called "OREO Speedwagon," but we've only got one chocolate guy and two vanilla crèmes. Do you know another black dude who can sing like me that can be our other chocolate?"

Kristi laughed and looked at me to see if I was going to say anything too. When I still couldn't, she had no choice but to break the bad news to us herself.

"Sorry guys, I hate to be the one to ruin your sing along, but that's *not* an REO Speedwagon song."

Hello, what's this? A Malenglish throw down, mano a mano…except it was three against one and the one was a girl? It would be like shooting fish in a barrel. But how would I correct her without looking like a "Chet"? I finally found my voice and went with the ever-so-subtle Kelly Leak method from the *Bad News Bears*.

"If you're right, then you get a 50% tip; if I'm right, you have to go on a date with me."

She looked at me as if I had just walked into a trap, while Alex and Jim looked at me as if I had just solved Fermat's last theorem. It was a genius move on my part for sure. They had true envy in their eyes.

"I really shouldn't," Kristi said coyly. "I'd hate to take away the money you need for singing lessons."

Oh Fudge! Except I didn't think "Fudge." This girl thought she had a black belt in Malenglish, and I needed to announce my presence with authority. Jim and Alex were just sitting there frozen in shock, so it was up to me to put a Scott Farkas style whuppin' on her.

"Do we have a bet?" I asked, "because I need to get on my cell phone and call my office to have someone go on-line and get the answer for us."

"Yes, it's a bet," Kristi replied, "and you can save the money on your phone bill because the name of the group is listed right beside the title of the song on the jukebox." She walked away from the table without looking back.

I was beginning to sense a feeling of dread creeping over me, but I tried to play it cool. Alex, on the other hand, was up like a cat and running over to the jukebox with Jim nipping at his heels. I knew my fears were confirmed when I saw both of them doing their best imitation of Fred Sanford having his "big one." Anyone walking into the place at that moment would have started CPR on them right away.

Finally they sauntered back to the table, shaking their heads and getting back on their stools.

"Santana," Alex said dejectedly. "Freakin' Santana."

"*I'm Winning*" – Santana, 1981

"Santana?" I asked incredulously. *"You've Got to Change Your Evil Ways,* Santana? *"She's a Black Magic Woman,* Santana? How does a band go from Mexican gypsy music to an '80's love ballad without us knowing about it?"

"I don't know, man. Sure fooled the crap out of me," Jim said. "But then again, I'm the black guy here. I blame you whiteys for choking on that one. Shoot, in 1981, Michael Jackson was the only music I was listening to. Of course, now he's gone and joined your team with the rest of you whiteys."

About that time, Kristi returned with our drink orders. To her credit, she took our food orders and didn't gloat about the victory. "I wouldn't have believed it either if I hadn't seen it on the jukebox a few days ago. But please be sure to order plenty of food so that my winnings are equivalent to what I would have lost. I'd hate to think that a date with Chuck was only worth four dollars," she said with a grin.

Jim was obviously a glutton for punishment, because he decided to make another run at Kristi. He was like the guy on *Tin Cup* who just *knew* that he could eventually make the shot.

"I like your Monarchs jersey," he said. "As you might imagine from looking at me, I'm a huge fan of the old Negro Leagues. So we'll go double-or-nothing on the bet if you can name one person who played for the Monarchs."

Kristi didn't even give me or Alex time to pull ourselves out of the bet. "How about the winningest pitcher in the history of professional baseball, Satchel Paige. Over *two thousand* wins in the Negro and Cuban leagues combined! Would he count?"

Once again she turned towards the kitchen without giving us time to get over our astonishment, but this time she paused and came back to the table.

"By the way," she stated, "why isn't it called the 'Satchel Paige Award' instead of the 'Cy Young Award' that they give out to the best pitcher every year? I'll tell you why. It's because Satchel Paige was black, and apparently my white ancestors were too narrow-minded to accept his greatness. It's just like the barbershop scene in *Coming to America* where Eddie Murphy's dressed up like the old black guy and he says that every time he mentions Joe Louis, some white guy starts screaming about how good Rocky Marciano was."

"Oh, and by the way," Kristi continued as she walked away, "be sure to save room for dessert; I can't afford for you guys to skip it now that I'm up to 100% on the dollar!"

Jim looked like he'd had his pants pulled down and been spanked on national television. If I had ever wondered whether a black man could turn red from embarrassment and pale from shock at the same time, I now knew it was possible. Kristi had just tugged on his cape *and* spit in the wind.

"You Don't Mess Around With Jim" – Jim Croce, 1972.

"Don't worry, it's just a flesh wound," Alex taunted Jim with a cockney accent.

"Good God, man," I chided Jim, "did you eat a lot of paint chips when you were a kid?"

"That's not a girl...that's a *man,* baby!" said Jim, looking like *Shaft* but sounding like *Austin Powers*.

I made a promise to myself, right then and there, that I would work up the courage to eventually ask Kristi out on a date. I knew, however, that the first thing I had to do was adequately prepare myself. I had heard the rumors and legendary tales through the grapevine about hot-looking women who spoke Malenglish, but I had never before encountered one. The result was clearly less than impressive on my part; I'd been out macho-ed by a girl.

Apparently landing one of these mythical nymphs with the brain of a man and the body of a woman was not going to be an easy undertaking. I couldn't catch the Loch Ness Monster with a cane pole, nor could I slay Bigfoot with a bottle rocket. It was going to take some serious research and preparation on my part before I was ready to go toe-to-toe with a creature that could melt my defense shields with her body and then slice me into a thousand pieces with her sharp Malenglish wit.

I shuddered. What was that? Why had I just felt a seismic shift in The Force? Why did baseball cards suddenly seem so irrelevant? I knew the rest of my afternoon had just been shot to hell.

Chapter 16

New York City
July, 2007

Joe Marinolli pulled out his trusty and tattered address book and flipped through the faded pages, looking for the name of that one particular baseball card expert that he'd been spoken to nearly a generation ago when had made the initial inquiries about his Frank Bowerman cards. He doubted that the guy was still at the same address or phone number, but Joe knew that he could locate him via the internet if he could just find his name. Granted, the guy may have quit messing with baseball cards as he'd aged and had probably gotten a real job of some sort by now, but at least it was a good place to start.

Ah, there it was: *"Barry Stone – baseball cards,"* scribbled in Joe's handwriting from his younger days when his penmanship wasn't affected by his essential tremors. Joe logged on to his laptop and Googled the name.

Good gracious! Not only was Stone still playing around with baseball cards, but he'd apparently turned into a full-time successful venture. His name was cited everywhere as an expert in the field of vintage cards, and he had his own auction site where various old cards were currently available.

Joe didn't see any Frank Bowerman cards as he scrolled through the present auction, but he did see several similar-looking cards that must have come from the same set. The website described them as being from the T-206 set, which did trigger a spark of recollection in Joe's mind, and they were selling for upwards of $800 each. Whoa, Joe thought to himself, maybe his pile of old Bowerman cards had some value after all.

He clicked over to EBay and ran a search for completed auctions on Bowerman T-206 cards. To his surprise and dismay, they were only selling in the forty dollar range. Pretty expensive for a bookmark, Joe chuckled, but he couldn't save Stratton Park at that rate.

Joe clicked back on the window that reopened the Google search on Barry Stone and found his business address. One of the luxuries of being 89-years old was that you had nowhere to go and no schedule to follow, so Joe decided that he'd call his private transportation service and have them deliver him, his wheelchair and his newfound sheet of cards to Barry Stone's shop in Brooklyn. It was a nice day outside anyways, and Joe wanted the company.

Joe's driver opened the door to Stone's shop so that Joe could wheel himself in through the door with the oversized sketch pad in his lap. The shop was empty at the time, other than an older man behind the counter who was looking at cards through a magnifying glass.

"Sir," Jim spoke, "will I be able to use your telephone to call my driver to come pick me up when I'm finished here?"

"Sure," the man replied, no problem."

"Okay, Dr. Joe, I'll be in this general vicinity anyways," the driver said, "so just give me a buzz and I'll probably be able to get here in fifteen minutes or so." Joe tipped the driver and thanked him as he left the store.

"Is there anything in particular I can help you with?" the man behind the counter asked.

"Are you by any chance Barry Stone?"

"In the flesh," he replied.

"I know you don't remember," Joe said, wheeling himself up to the counter to shake Stone's hand, "but you gave me some good honest advice over the phone many, many years ago, so I wanted to come back to you for more advice on the same type of subject. I'm Dr. Joe Marinolli, but please just call me Joe."

"Okay Joe, will do, but please call me Barry as well," Stone said cheerfully. "Yeah, I've lost a lot of deals over the years in this hobby by being honest and forthright, but I've found that the rewards seem to come in the end. A lot of unscrupulous people have come and gone from the baseball card collecting business, and unfortunately too many unsuspecting people have fallen prey to these card sharks.

I couldn't sleep at night if I knew that I had ripped off some widow by paying her a hundred dollars for a ten thousand dollar card. The way I look at it, when someone comes to me asking for an appraisal, I then have a fiduciary duty to give that person my honest assessment. If they want to then sell it to me for a tiny bit less so that I can turn around and sell it for a marginal profit, that's fine. I've got to pay the overhead somehow. But ripping people off is not my style."

Joe knew that he had made the right decision in coming to this place. He pulled the uncut cardboard sheet out of the sketch pad very gingerly and laid it carefully on top of the glass display case. "Very well then, Barry, can I please retain your services to give me an estimate on this?"

Stone glanced at what Joe had laid on the counter and then gazed back at Joe with a sympathetic look on his face. "I'm sorry, Joe, but I hope you didn't pay too much for this. We see these almost every day, so I hope you weren't the victim of a scam. How much did you pay for these Wagner reprints?"

Joe was befuddled. *Wagner*? What made Wagner any different than Kling or Brown or Bowerman? Joe wondered.

"I'm truly sorry that I don't know what this thing's worth, Barry, but the good news is that I didn't pay a dime for it. I actually found it last night in an old footlocker that belonged to my father when he was a child, along with this." Joe handed him the old pay stub from the American Lithograph Company.

Stone glanced at it, and then read it again slower.

"So the Marinolli on this receipt was your father?" he asked. Joe nodded. Stone picked his magnifying glass back up and started examining the cardboard sheet of cards a little closer this time. He turned it over and started examining the back as well.

Finally, after what seemed like an eternity to Joe, Stone looked up at him, and then looked around the store as if he had just awoken from a trance and was unfamiliar with his surroundings. Without saying a word, Stone hurried over and locked the door, pulling down the shade and turning the sign on the door to "Closed" in the process.

"You don't need to shut down just to talk to me, Barry. I don't want you to lose any business in the meantime," Joe offered.

"I didn't shut that door to *talk* to you," Stone said, visibly shaking, "I shut it to *protect* us both!"

Chapter 17

Brooklyn, New York
2007

"Who have you shown this to?" Stone asked nervously. "Does your driver know about it? Have you called any other baseball card stores about it?"

"No," Joe said, starting to get a bit worried.

"Phew, that's good," Stone said as he exhaled deeply with a big sigh of relief. "That's *real* good." Stone reached under into a box of latex gloves and slipped a pair on his hands.

"You really don't know what this is, do you Joe?" he asked. "Or is this *Candid Camera* and you've got a hidden camera on that wheelchair somewhere? That's what's going on, right?"

Joe was beginning to think that Stone was losing his mind. "No, Barry, I *don't* know what it is, and I'm not the type of guy who likes playing cruel jokes on people. Maybe I *should* just take it to somebody else."

"No, no!" Stone exclaimed loudly. "That's the *last* thing you want to do. I'm sorry if I offended you, but let me take a few minutes to tell you some things and then I think you'll see where I'm coming from."

Joe sat back in his wheelchair and listened as Stone began to speak again.

"I still need to do a lot more thorough examination, Joe, but what this appears to be is an uncut sheet of cards from the T-206 tobacco set from 1909. That's the obvious part that you had probably already figured out yourself. Here's what you apparently don't know. First of all, do you even know who Honus Wagner is?"

Joe admitted that the name rang a bell, but that he really had never followed professional baseball. Stone continued with his lecture.

"It turns out that Wagner was one of the greatest shortstops of all time, voted into the baseball hall of fame in their inaugural class in 1936 along with Ty Cobb, Christy Mathewson, Walter Johnson and some guy you probably *have* heard of named Babe Ruth. But that's not why his T-206 card is so valuable. They're valuable because he apparently did not give them permission to use his image, so very few of them were ever made.

These other four players on the sheet are nice players -- Brown and Young were also voted into the Hall of Fame later on – but their cards are pretty easily found since large quantity of them were put into circulation back then. The Wagners were never supposed to get into circulation, so they have always been a 'chase card,' which is what those of us in the hobby call the one card from any set that everyone always seems to be lacking."

The light finally went on in Joe's head as the fog lifted, and he could remember with clarity now the initial conversation that he'd had with Barry Stone some forty years ago.

"Holy smokes," Joe said eagerly, "that's what you told me forty years ago when I called you the first time. I had asked you about the value of my old Frank Bowerman cards, and you had mentioned that the *real* valuable cards from that set were the Wagner cards. That was somewhere around 1968, and you told me that Wagners were worth about $250 each!"

Stone laughed. "Well, I was right at the time. What I didn't know was how much they would appreciate from there. Nowadays a very low-grade example sells for $150,000 or more. The best-known Wagner just sold for $2,500,000 at public auction -- I should know since I was the one who bought it for one of my clients – and it has already been resold for even more than that."

"But I guess I should rephrase that," Stone said with a grin. "That could only have been the *seventh-best* T-206 Wagner in existence…because I'm staring at *six* gem mint beauties that absolutely blow that one out of the water!"

Joe was dumbfounded. His heart started racing and he was finding it hard to breathe. He couldn't believe what he was hearing.

"On top of everything I just mentioned, nobody in the history of card collecting has ever been able to find an uncut sheet of T-206 cards, and believe me, they've searched everywhere. The closest thing anyone has ever found was a strip of five cards – the same five cards on your sheet, in fact: Brown, Wagner, Bowerman, Young and Kling.

That strip of cards was supposedly found in the pocket of an old jacket belonging to Honus Wagner himself, and it just sold recently for $250,000 or so. So, even if you had found an uncut sheet of T-206 cards with thirty players on it who had never done anything but ride the pine, the value of that one-of-a-kind sheet would still be in the $500,000 range. But for you to have an uncut sheet with *six Wagners* on it? The sky's the limit."

Stone pulled off his gloves and turned back to Joe. "Joe, if you had shown this sheet to anyone else, they would have paid you $5,000 for it and you would have thought you won the lottery. I don't know what you've done in life to have God smile on you and send you into my shop, but it must have been good."

"And," Stone continued, "you've helped me realize what a good person I really am, because if there was ever a time when I would be tempted to kill someone and make away with millions of dollars that could never be traced, this would be it!"

But as it turned out, Stone may have killed him after all, because Joe's heart attack was in full bloom by then!

Chapter 18

Atlanta
2007

Kristi and I were on our first date, and things couldn't have been going better. Now that she was all dolled up, she was a stunner. Every guy in the restaurant was eyeing her as we walked to our table, but most of them were probably convincing themselves that she was a bitch or a psycho. That's how men cope with seeing someone else with a hot girlfriend.

The best thing for me was that everyone could see her slim figure and long legs in the dress she was wearing. At least this eliminated the "iceberg effect" as one of the natural assumptions to be made by the jealous fellas that were wondering why a girl like this was with me and not with them.

If you speak Malenglish, then you already know that the "iceberg effect" is familiar danger for men lurking in bars trying to pick up women. I guess technically it might work the same way in reverse, but I don't know since I've never discussed it with a woman. Essentially, there is a well-known principle of physics that says only 10% of an iceberg shows above the surface, while the much larger mass lurks unseen below.

The same laws of nature that apply to icebergs apparently apply to certain women. It is not uncommon for a guy to meet an attractive girl sitting at a table with her friends and him to ask her for a dance, only to realize that what he could see above the table was only a small portion of what she held in store for him. Her face was pretty, but when she got up her butt looked like two bulldogs in cellophane wrap fighting for a bone. Many a "cruiser" had been sunk for the night after running into one of these icebergs.

Kristi could not have chosen a better place for our date, a Brazilian steakhouse in Buckhead named Fogo de Chao, where for all intents and purposes you could literally eat different cuts of meat until you exploded. I made a mental note *not* to partake in the after dinner mint. The catch, of course, was not to indulge in the world-class salad bar or the steaming hot muffins that were served prior to the gorging. If they could trick you into wasting stomach space on those filler items, then you would eat less meat and their profit margins would soar.

Their other ploy is to bring around the cuts of sirloin and tout them as the "house special." It takes a wise and patient man to turn them away and wait for the guy with the cuts of filet mignon to come around, but eventually the maitre de waves the white flag when he realizes that you're on to their shenanigans and he sends the tenderloin over to your table. Then it's "game on" at that point; the only reason to stop being that you've swallowed your fork or eaten your napkin.

"You really look spectacular tonight," I said, trying my best to repress my Malenglish brogue and speak nothing but pure Female.

"Are you talking to me or that big leg of lamb that just went by?" Kristi asked with a giggle.

I laughed. "Hey, it could be worse. Some guys have roaming eyes for other women; I have roaming eyes for carcasses of beef and pork."

Kristi really opened up to me, bringing me up to speed on her parents and her upbringing. She was not embarrassed to mention that her parents were both educators back home outside of Knoxville, and that therefore she had not lead a very privileged life. She had made honor roll in high school, but could not afford college and had been working for ten years now to try and save up enough to enroll somewhere. She was finally getting close to her goal.

All in all, Kristi was extremely confident and comfortable with who she was and where she came from. It was refreshing to finally meet someone who wasn't trying to put on a false front and pretend to be something they weren't. I found myself becoming very attracted to her for what she was on the *inside*.

How's *that* for sounding like a female, huh? Okay, I'm not going to lie to you; the smoking hot package on the *outside* wasn't hurting matters either.

Somewhere between ingesting my second and third pound of succulent meat, I managed to bring Kristi up to speed on my recent baseball card experience. As I should have expected, she was fully aware that Honus Wagner's card was the sacred prize of the collecting world. Her brothers had collected cards when she was growing up, so she had heard about the fabled card many times over.

As the evening was drawing to a close, I found a parking space on the street outside Kristi's apartment building and walked her to the door. I had been dying to kiss her all night, and probably would've had butterflies in my stomach if there'd been any room for them next to the slab of beef I was carrying in there. My belly was stretched so tight I felt like I was due to deliver twins at any moment.

As we approached the stoop, Kristi stopped to get her key out of her purse. "Do you want to come up and see my baseball card collection?" she asked with a twinkle in her eye. "It shouldn't take very long, since there aren't any cards. Then maybe afterwards we could snuggle on the couch and watch a romantic musical, like *Spinal Tap* or *School of Rock.*"

Uh oh, that did it. Now my belly wasn't the only place where my skin was stretched tight. *Schwing*!

But wait a minute. Maybe this is just a test? Maybe I'm supposed to decline the offer and look like a chivalrous gentleman?

Good Lord! What the hell was I thinking? Who had crawled inside my head for a moment – John Boy Freakin' Walton? I reminded myself of the slogan that I had chosen to live by for years after seeing all of those "What Would Jesus Do?" bracelets that were so popular.

My acronym was just a wee bit more secular; I lived to the WWWD creed. And as I bounded up the stairs behind Kristi, I knew *exactly* what Wilt Would Do!

Holy smokes, my internal Chuck Evans iPod was playing a song that it had never played before:

"Chuck E.'s In Love" – Ricky Lee Jones, 1979.

Chapter 19

Brooklyn, New York
2007

Joe Marinolli was on a raft, floating on a peaceful river in a dense fog. He could hear the gentle chirping of crickets and the murmur of rushing water as the sun started to rise and the haze started to lift.

"Joe, can you hear me? It's me, Tom Bennett, from the orphanage," he said, coming closer. "Can you hear me now?"

Joe was able to barely nod his head, finding it humorous to himself that he had been brought back from the dead by a cell phone commercial.

"Thank God you made it! You're at the New York Methodist Hospital in Brooklyn. Apparently you had a heart attack. Boy, you sure had all of us at the orphanage worried like crazy, especially the kids."

As Joe's eyes became accustomed to the light, he looked around the room and noticed hundreds of "Get Well Soon" cards that the children at the orphanage had made for him by hand. If there was ever any doubt that he would give his last cent to help those kids, it was gone now.

Oh no! Speaking of helping the orphanage and "gone now," Joe remembered where he had been before being stricken and started to panic about whether or not his cards were accounted for. Or had he just dreamed the whole thing? The beeping noise on his heart monitor started to speed up.

"Joe, Joe, calm down! Relax! I'll go get a nurse!" said Tom as he charged out of the room.

As Joe watched Tom leave the room, he perceived someone else seated in the room. He felt a wave of relief come over him.

"Hey Joe, it's me, Barry," Stone said as he stood from his chair. "You sure scared the crap out of me, pulling that stunt in my store like that! Luckily 911 was able to get someone over there immediately and they rushed you here. The doctor says you're gonna be okay, but you may have to stay here for a while."

Joe tried to thank him, but was barely able to speak with a tube down his throat. "Annnnnx," Joe croaked.

"Don't mention it," Stone said, grabbing Joe's hand and squeezing firmly. "And whatever you do, do *not* worry about your baseball cards. I locked everything in my safe at the store while I was waiting for the ambulance to arrive, and have since transferred them to the largest safe deposit box available at the Bank of America right around the corner. They're not going *anywhere* until you are ready for them to do so."

"Annnnnx," Joe croaked again.

"But whatever you do," Stone reminded him, "do *not* breathe a word of this to anyone. A dozen people a day get killed in this city for a lot less than $500,000. From everything I can figure, the market value for your gem mint full uncut sheet of T-206 cards with six Wagners on it is worth a *minimum* of $10 million and probably closer to twice that much."

Upon hearing this, Joe instinctively squeezed Stone's hand so tight that he almost lost circulation.

"I know, Joe, I know. It's unbelievable, isn't it? But I've collected baseball cards for over a half-century and never thought that I would see the day that something like this would surface. And this thing is so big that it will transcend just the baseball card world; this thing will rival the great works of art or the rarest archeological finds.

There are people who have never even heard of baseball who will pay millions just to own it because it's so rare and so desirable. I'm thinking that we should publicize the auction for several months, get some appearances on network TV, do the whole media hype thing. This will really get the bidders into frenzy. Then an auction in December of this year will be the biggest event of the season."

Joe wanted desperately to speak, but he couldn't do anything but gag and cough. He made a writing motion with his hand, and Stone grabbed him a pen and note pad.

"No auction," Joe wrote. *"Sell fast. Proceeds to orphanage before park's gone."*

Stone was noticeably disappointed at the prospect of losing the biggest auction in memorabilia history, but he wasn't deterred. "I guess you're referring to Stratton Park. While we were waiting for you to come around, Tom told me about the park and how sad it's going to be for all the children if the bank forecloses on the note. I guess that's why time is of the essence, huh?"

Joe nodded ever so slightly.

"Well, let me see what I can do. Here's the thing, Joe. I can think of one place right now that would pay a pretty penny for the sheet. They paid through the nose for the Wagner card that I just sold to them on behalf of my client, and I know they have a serious interest in buying every T-206 Wagner card they can.

But -- and this may not mean a thing to you, but it means a lot to me because I'm a sentimental old fart -- I've been led to believe that this buyer will actually destroy the cards as soon as they get them. I know it sounds ridiculous, but they've got their reasons and I'll explain them to you in more detail later. But nonetheless, once you sold the sheet, it would cease to exist forever."

Joe shook his head back and forth. "Uhhh uhhhh," he moaned, once again asking for a pen. He wrote: *"They were my dad's. Can't destroy his legacy."*

"Okay, I agree," Stone said, "but it may be that they're the only ones who will pay the type of money we're talking about in a fast enough money to save the park. How about I at least talk to them and see what they offer?"

Joe nodded his approval.

"And there's one other person that I think you need to meet," Stone said with a smile. "I know you're not much of a baseball fan, but I think even *you* will recognize this name!"

Chapter 20

Atlanta
2007

Kristi and I had become a pretty regular item, and I have to admit that I was feeling emotions that I'd never thought possible for a macho male like me. Then again, when you're kissing your girlfriend and *she's* the one who breaks off the kiss because *SportsCenter's Top 10 Plays* is about to come on, it's not hard to fall in love.

I was sitting in my office staring out the window when Alex walked in and grabbed my suit jacket off the doorknob. Alex is easily 100 pounds heavier than I am (yes, even *after* the Brazilian steakhouse), so I knew what was coming but never ceased to laugh at it.

"Fat guy in a little coat. Fat guy in a little coat," Alex sang, looking just like Chris Farley in *Tommy Boy*.

"You looked like Jack Handey lost in a deep thought, so I just thought you needed some loosening up, Chuck," Alex laughed.

"Heh…heh,heh; you said upchuck," I said, knowing that my Malenglish license would be suspended if I missed a *Beavis & Butthead* opportunity that obvious.

Just then, my intercom buzzed. "Mr. Evans, there's a call for you on line three; a Mr. Stone. Do you want to take the call?"

"Yeah, Angie, I'll take it," I said, motioning for Alex to come in and shut the door behind him. I had no idea why Stone was calling me back, but I was wondering if maybe his deal with Duke had gone south.

"Hello again, Mr. Stone. To what do I owe this pleasure?" I asked.

"Mr. Evans, before I let you in on an interesting turn of events, I need to know that everything I tell you is going to be held in strict confidence. Is there a way that we can enter into an attorney-client arrangement so that my information is privileged and you can only release it to certain individuals at my direction?"

"That all depends," I replied. "I need to know a little more information. For starters, I can't agree to represent you if your matter is in conflict with anything I have going with an existing client."

"Actually," Stone interrupted, "It's quite the opposite. Your current client would actually benefit greatly from this arrangement, and he is one of the people to whom I intend to allow you full discretion to share the information. Provided, of course, that he will also agree to keep it confidential. Trust me, it will be in your client's best interest *not* to share this information with another living soul."

"Well, unless I'm dumber than Navin R. Johnson, it sounds to me like you have a lead on another T-206 Wagner card, Mr. Stone," I said. "If that's correct, and the only way you will talk to me about it is for me to represent you, then I think we can work it out. As long as you know up front that I represent Jerry Johns and will still be working as his agent and trying to get him the best price I can on the card. I simply cannot agree to hide anything from him or do anything to harm his interests at all."

Stone accepted these terms and agreed to let me draw up a contract for representation and send it to him via fax. He also agreed to let me reach The Big Stick by phone and get his permission for the arrangement. An hour later the signed copy of our standard contract had been faxed back by Stone and the Stickman was more excited than ever, so I called Stone back to take up where we had left off earlier.

"Okay, Chuck. Can I call you Chuck now that you're my lawyer?" Stone laughed.

"No," I replied, "now only 'sire' or 'your highness' will suffice. Yes, of course you can call me Chuck, Barry."

"*May-bel-line...*" Stone started singing without hesitating a bit. He was clearly a Malenglish Mensa.

"Good one," I said with respect. "Too bad your first name isn't Norris, or you could have kung fu'd my ass in half over the telephone!"

"Carl Douglas," Stone said matter-of-factly.

"Carl Douglas?" I queried. "Who's Carl Douglas?"

"Carl Douglas, *Everybody Was Kung Fu Fighting*, 1974," Stone said, as if I was a mental midget.

Damn! This guy was good. Clearly spending his life around baseball cards had given him *plenty* of time to speak Malenglish *far away* from the presence of any ladies.

"Wow, Barry nice," I joked.

"Yeah, I definitely appreciate a sense of humor, Chuck, but what I'm about to tell you is as serious as it gets. It's the biggest thing I've ever been involved with, and I suspect the same may be true for you as well."

My interest was certainly peaked. "Go on," I said.

"First of all, let's just say that I look like a genius for advising my previous client to sell his Wagner to the Duke University Foundation. That card was priced so high because it was the best-known example in existence. Well, believe it or not, another Wagner has surfaced that is in even better condition."

"Oh man," I gasped, "the Stick is going to think I'm the schizzle or the snizzle or whatever it is that means I'm cool these days! But holy cow, what is this one going for?"

"Actually," Stone said slowly, drawing it out, "it's *six* mint condition Wagners, all on one uncut sheet of cards straight from the factory."

"Oh. My. God."

"That's pretty much what I said when they came into my store. I still keep hearing Bogie in the back of my mind saying '*Of all the card joints in all the towns in all the world, they came into mine*'."

"So who brought 'em in?" I asked eagerly. "Hopefully not someone up there from one of those mob counterfeiting rings we see so many movies about."

"No, *they're real, and they're spectacular,*" Stone deadpanned. Where would Malenglish be without *Seinfeld*? How did people even communicate back then?

Stone continued. "An elderly gentleman brought them to me and was in the process of retaining my services to sell them for him when he had a heart attack in my store. He's in the hospital now and is recovering nicely, but he may not have long to live. More importantly, the reason he is selling them is that he wants to come up with several million dollars to donate to an orphanage here in New York where he spends a lot of time volunteering to read to the children.

Apparently he's done it for decades because he never married or had any kids of his own. The kids in the orphanage are like his own, and they're going to lose the park where they currently play baseball and other activities if they don't come up with a big chunk of change in the immediate future. So it turns out that this sheet of Wagner cards is the answer to all of their prayers."

"Okay, so how is this any different than your last experience?" I asked. "Why not just call the folks at Duke again and get the orphanage paid off in no time? And why would I want to let Jerry Johns buy the thing if it runs the same risk that we talked about before of being forfeited in lawsuit?"

"That's where it gets almost magical, Chuck. Seriously. It turns out that the old guy who now owns the sheet, Dr. Joe Marinolli, is the son of the original owner. He found the sheet tucked away at the bottom of his father's old trunk. So the provenance of this item is second-to-none."

"Okay," I interjected, "but what's to stop Duke from coming after the sheet as property of the American Tobacco Company and James Duke's estate? And what's to stop any of the Wagner relatives from claiming royalties like we talked about before?"

"Bear with me, Chuck," Stone said patiently, "and you'll see it all clearly in a minute. Remember, the law in 1909 only prohibited the tobacco company from using Wagner's image *for profit* without his permission. The only way they made profit was from selling cigarettes, so therefore the only way a T-206 card could have made a profit for the tobacco company was if it was actually inserted and sold with a pack of smokes.

These cards are *uncut,* so there is *no way* they could have been inserted in a pack and sold. Accordingly, because they were never used for anything, no long-lost Wagner relative could ever argue that these particular examples were used *for profit.*"

"*Excellent, Smithers, excellent,*" I sneered. "But wait! If these were never inserted into packs, then aren't they still technically the property of the tobacco company? Can't Duke come after them under that theory?"

"Ah, but there's more!" Stone said rapidly. "Remember, the tobacco company never got permission from Wagner to use the cards in their product, so they cancelled the print order for Wagner cards altogether. They never paid the printer for the job and they never received the cards.

That's the position Duke will *have* to take, because it's by far the safest for them. If they maintain that they never even received the cards from the printer, then it will completely bar any claim for past lost profits from any Wagner descendants because it would prove that they could never have used the cards for profit."

"Wow," I said in amazement. "Is there any chance that the American Lithograph Company still exists and that *they* could make an ownership claim to the sheet of cards?"

"No, and No," Stone said confidently. "First of all, the company went under in the Great Depression and left no remaining entity behind. Second, along with the sheet of cards, Dr. Marinolli also found a pay stub that proves his father was an *employee* of the American Lithograph Company at the time these cards were printed.

We know that the print order for these cards was cancelled, and we know that the American Lithograph

Company had no permission from Wagner to use the cards for any purpose of theirs, so the only logical assumption is that the cards became "printer's scrap" that was thrown into the trash. Or given away for free to employees like Mr. Marinolli's father.

Either way, since there is no law against an employee taking something home for himself once his employer has thrown it away, Mr. Marinolli's father would be the lawful owner of the uncut sheet."

I was speechless. It was perfect. I could only think of one last question. "If there is no way that the sheet of cards can be used by any of Wagner's relatives to bring a multi-million dollar case against the tobacco trust, then why would Duke have any interest in it?"

"I'll give you ten seconds to think about it, Chuck, and I'm sure it will come to you." It did with six seconds to spare.

"Duke wants them," I offered, "because otherwise someone could buy the sheet and cut the cards off, thereby creating *six separate* cards that someone could use as evidence in *six separate* lawsuits for lost profits. The danger to Duke is an individual card that could possibly have been inserted in a pack of cigs. They want to get these and destroy them before this happens."

"Ding, Ding, Ding; we have a winner! You win the grand prize. You get the leg lamp...or this ashtray...or this paddle game...or this remote control," Stone joked. "Sorry for the giddiness, Chuck, but this really is the greatest find since the Family Truckster."

"But this all brings me right back to where I started, Barry," I said, "which is wondering why you don't just call Duke and sell it to them?"

"This sheet of cards is the only remaining link between Dr. Marinolli and the father that he never knew. His father was killed in World War One when he was only a few months old, so this sheet of cards is precious to him. If it wasn't for those kids at the orphanage, he wouldn't even *think* about selling it.

But believe it or not, his dad was actually raised at the *same orphanage* where the money is going – the New York Foundling Orphanage. So he feels as if his dad would want him to sell the cards to benefit the kids, but *not* to someone who is going to immediately *destroy* them. In the end, however, saving the park is the number one goal. Therefore, if we have no other legitimate buyers, then Duke will get them."

"So I guess the whole point of this conversation is for you to educate me so that I can educate the Big Stick so that we can see if he is interested in being that legitimate buyer, huh?" I asked.

"Sure it is, Chuck," Stone admitted, "but think of how great it will look for Jerry Johns to buy a piece of national history at an extremely high price when 100% of the money is going to charity. If we spin this right, both Dr. Joe Marinolli, Jr. and Mr. Jerry "The Big Stick" Johns are going to come across as national heroes!"

Stone was right. This was a "can't miss" proposition. Or was it too good to be true? I promised Stone that I would discuss the matter with the Stickman and get back to him as soon as possible.

Jerry Johns finally got around to returning my call late that afternoon.

"Now *that's* what I'm talkin' about, little Chuck!" Johns shouted excitedly. "Why buy one card when you can get the whole damn sheet! I don't care what you have to pay for it, you just go buy me that sheet! I knew it was good omen that your dad was out of the country to where he couldn't be reached. He would be talking about the wisdom and security of tax-free bonds and all that boring crap.

I told him one time, 'I'm the *real* home run king of this sport, not that other guy, so I don't want *nothin'* that's got the word *Bonds* associated with it!' I don't even think he got the joke, he's such a tight-ass.

Anyway, you're younger and got more balls, so I know you'll close this deal out for me. You're 'Wonderboy,' just like that bat from *The Natural*. Now just go out there and don't crack under pressure like 'Wonderboy' did...or I'll be looking for a new agent. I'll have Bobby pick me a winner, if you catch my drift." He hung up without waiting to hear my answer.

Okay, simple enough. I had a bag full of cash and it was time to go shopping!

"Papa's Got a Brand New Bag" – James Brown, 1965.

Chapter 21

Atlanta
2007

Now *this* is a weird dream.

I am actually *in* the movie *Ferris Bueller's Day Off*, and I'm sitting in Cameron's car next to him. He's wearing his Detroit Red Wings Gordie Howe jersey, gripping the wheel and grimacing, as he says, "he'll keep calling me."

I hear a phone ring, and then Cameron says it again with his teeth clenched tight: "he'll keep calling me."

Once again I hear a phone ring, then Cameron shakes his head in frustration and says, "he'll make me feel guilty."

Now I hear a third ring of the phone, and Cameron hauls off and kicks me! What the hell – this wasn't in the movie! He's kicking me hard, right in the small of my back!

Finally I open my eyes to escape the attack from Gordie Howe turned goon.

"Jeez, get the phone, Chuck," Kristi says as she's booting me with her foot and pulling the covers up over her head. "Nobody calls this late unless it's bad news. And it's gonna be bad news for *you* if that's an old girlfriend calling at this hour."

I look over at the clock and see that it's 3:37 in the morning. Kristi and I had fallen asleep watching *The Naked Gun* on one of those old movie channels, and sure enough, Ferris and Cameron were on the screen now, screwing around with Ed Rooney. Thank God it hadn't been a horror film on, or Kristi might have woken me up with a chainsaw or machete.

I grabbed the phone and said something that came out sounding like "muh."

"Is this Chuck Evans, Jr.; the attorney?" asked the caller urgently.

"Yeah, and this had better be Ed Freakin' McMahon," I replied angrily. Inside, however, I was feeling fortunate that it really *hadn't* been an old girlfriend calling. I've dated a few that liked to boil rabbits, if you know what I mean.

"Chuck, it's me, Barry Stone, and I'm sorry to be calling you this late, but it's an emergency. My store just got firebombed!"

"Holy shit!" I exclaimed as I hopped out of bed and went into the other room to talk. "Are they sure it was a bomb and not a gas leak or something?"

"Yeah, the arson guys said that there's no doubt that chemical explosives were used. Unfortunately, as you might expect, they suspect *me* for torching the place so that I can make an insurance claim."

"Aw crap," I said softly, realizing that this was standard investigatory procedure for any business that burns down in the middle of the night. "But why would they think you would destroy all of your inventory only to get back exactly what it was worth? You'd been in business for thirty years at that location, so it's not like you were hemorrhaging money and about to go belly up."

"Well, that's where I may have screwed up. I got the call from the fire department to come down to my store, and the first thing I think to myself is 'thank heavens I have the safe' since all of my high dollar items are in the safe at night, and the damn thing is supposed to be fireproof and waterproof.

So as I'm driving to the store, I ask the arson guy over my cell phone how the safe fared and whether it survived intact. And the guy says, 'What safe?' Turns out the whole damn thing is *gone*! Whoever blew the place up may have wanted to cover it up, but there is no doubt that they stole the safe before torching the place."

"Ouch. No wonder they think you did it," I said sadly. "The main thing they look for in arson investigations is whether or not the owner removed any of his valuables from the premises before the fire. Now that they know you had a safe and that it's missing, you can bet that your insurance company will do everything possible to avoid paying your claim. They'll be convinced that you still have the cards and are trying to bilk them."

"Great. Just great. Can you get me an attorney up here who can defend me in this mess?" Stone pleaded.

"Sure thing. I'll do it first thing in the morning," I assured him.

"You know what this all means, don't you Chuck," Stone said in a whisper that I could barely hear. "It means that there was a leak all right, but it wasn't a gas leak – it was an *information* leak. Besides you and me, the Chairman of the Duke Foundation is the only other person who I told about the uncut Wagner sheet.

That safe I had easily weighed 750 pounds. Whoever hit my store couldn't have just made the decision to take it on the spur of the moment. It would take special equipment and plenty of manpower to do it quickly. There's no doubt in my mind that the target in this whole thing was the safe. And there's no doubt in my mind that whoever took the safe was trying to get the uncut sheet of cards."

"Damn, you're right," I said, "those stupid Duke people have gone too far this time. We'll nail their asses! You be sure to tell the arson investigators about this crap so that they can chase down the *real* suspects."

"Well, that's what I wanted to talk to you about, Chuck," Stone said carefully. "First of all, that would mean that they're going to suspect you and your people as well. I don't mean to offend you, but who else knew on your end?"

"Just my two associates, Alex and Jim, but I trust those guys with my life. Plus, we'd have no reason to leak the information, since keeping this thing under wraps was our main objective. That *last* thing we would do is tell anyone and run the risk of screwing our client out of his card."

"I know, I believe you," Stone said, "or we wouldn't be having this conversation. But here's the other part. If I have to start explaining this whole thing to the arson people, then I can assure you that the whole world will soon find out about the existence of this sheet. If someone was willing to blow up my business when only *two* people know about it, how much danger will my client and I be in when *everyone* knows about it?"

"Man, I hadn't thought of that," I admitted. I also knew selfishly that I didn't want the news of the find to go public, since that would certainly make it tougher for my client to end up with the card. "Okay, I agree, keep that part out of your conversations with the fire investigators for now. In fact, don't say another word to them until you've spoken with the lawyer I'm going to hook you up with in the morning. You and I are the only ones who *know* that it was someone from Duke or on their payroll who did this, so let's just store that information away and save it for the right time."

"Sounds like a good plan," Stone said. "But you do realize, don't you, that as soon as the thieves get that safe opened, they're going to be extremely pissed off that the T-206 Wagners aren't there. Duke is going to send someone else after me; I'm a marked man!"

"Don't panic," I said, trying to sound calm myself. "When I call the attorney in the morning, I'll explain the situation to him without going into specifics and I'll get him to hire a bodyguard for you. There's no shortage of good ones up there."

"Thanks, I really appreciate it. I'm even afraid to go home now, so I think I'll drive over to my sister's place and crash there until the morning. Call me on my cell when you speak to the attorney, okay?"

Stone gave me his cell number and we ended the call. I knew that I wasn't going to be able to go back to sleep either after all this excitement, so I threw on a t-shirt and a pair of jeans and decided to head to the office for an early start. I'd be coming back in a few hours to wake up Kristi, so I'd change into my work clothes then after a little Starbucks break.

"Black Coffee In Bed" – Squeeze, 1982.

Chapter 22

Atlanta
2007

I parked my car in the deserted parking garage and stuck my elevator key into the slot that would enable me to exit at the main lobby floor of our building. I would have to go through security at that point and then get on the main elevators to go up to our floors. I didn't have my lanyard around my neck because I refused to wear it and look like a geek at a Trekkie Convention, but it was no problem since the night watchman had known me since I was a kid coming to my dad's office.

"Up early today, Mr. Chuck," Ernest said with a grin, "I thought your dad wasn't coming back for another week or two?"

"Funny; real funny," I joked back. "I'll be sure to tell him you were dead-ass asleep down here when I came in."

"Oh no sir, Mr. Chuck," Ernest pantomimed, breaking into a great Uncle Remus, "whatever you do, don't throw me in the briar patch!"

I laughed and headed toward the elevators.

"Hey Mr. Chuck!" Ernest called to me as I was about to push the button. "I was sorry to see Mr. Alex leave the firm. He was a good kid. I know you and him was tight, so I know you're probably sorry about it too."

The bell went off signifying that the elevator was arriving, but I ignored it and went back to Ernest's station. "What are you talking about, Ernest? I seriously don't know."

"Oh I'm so sorry to be the one to tell you then," he said sadly, "but I figured you knew. Mr. Alex was just down here a few hours ago, about midnight, and he left through here with a big box of all his personal stuff; pictures and trophies and so forth.

I joked with him, asking him why he had finally decided to take all his stuff to Goodwill and clean up his office, but I could tell he wasn't in no joking mood. He looked like his dog had just been run over, and he told me that he was leaving the firm. I just assumed he would have told you about it, since ya'll were such good friends and all."

I had already started running for the elevators as Ernest was finishing his thought. I didn't like where my mind was going, and I was praying that there was some other explanation for it. As the elevator reached our floor, I flew out and raced towards Alex's office. When I pushed open his door and flipped on the lights, it was completely bare. His diplomas were missing from the wall, and all of his personal items were gone. And worst of all – just as I had feared –

there was no note on his desk. He had just vanished in the night without a trace.

I went into my office and logged on, checking to see if Alex had sent me an e-mail explaining the situation.

Nothing.

What the hell? I knew there had to be something really big behind all of this, but what could have done it? Had Alex been having an improper affair with one of the staff and was now leaving to avoid being busted?

Or worse, had he been preparing this for a while and stolen some of our valuable clients in the process? I made a note to instruct every attorney to get on the phone in the morning and touch base with their clients, if for nothing else other than to bond. I also made a note to call New York and make arrangements for criminal representation for Barry Stone.

Then it hit me, and I felt like I had just been dropped off the *Tower of Terror*. I almost threw up, and instantly broke out in a cold sweat. Alex was the leak!

It was the only explanation that made sense. He knew everything about the sheet of cards and who had found it, but I had never told him or Jim about Stone moving the cards to a safe deposit box at his bank. Alex would have assumed that the cards were still at Stone's office, and he knew full well how valuable they were. He had sold out to his alma mater after all, that son of a bitch!

But wait a minute? Stone had already talked to the Duke Foundation himself, so they wouldn't need Alex to give them any special information. Crap! This meant that Alex had gone out into the open market with his information and sold it to someone for a bounty. He'd done all the research on the T-206 Wagner card for us, so he certainly would have come across the names of some "heavy hitters" who were chasing this card. The bastard had sold us down the river for some filthy lucre!

It was definitely CYA time on the old home front. Our firm had a client to whom we had sworn secrecy, and now one of our lawyers had violated that sacred privilege and caused our client to perhaps lose his business and be jailed for insurance fraud? Maybe my dad had the right idea about leaving the country; I should just join him over there and never come back.

I mulled over the situation and whether or not I needed to tell Barry about the news. There was absolutely no evidence or hard proof that Alex did anything wrong. Sure, his unexplained flight made him *look* guilty, but that wouldn't be enough to make any charges stick. Unless Alex flat out admitted it later – which no one would ever do -- there would never be any way of proving that the leak came from Alex and not from all the people involved with Duke University. Granted, nobody at Duke would have any reason to leak the information to a third party either, but at least it gave us a defense to any malpractice claim that Stone might bring.

Plus, Stone still had the sheet of cards tucked away safe and sound, so actually Alex's actions of bringing another big spender to the table would *benefit* Stone by raising the price of the card. Which, of course, would mean that the Big Stick could potentially end up paying more for the card than he would have had Alex kept his trap shut. So it was Jerry Johns that would have the malpractice suit against us.

Holy shit, that would be the end of the firm! I started to think that maybe it would be best if Johns *didn't* end up buying the card.

The best solution that I could come up with was to go ahead and terminate our representation of Barry Stone and move forward on the Big Stick's behalf. This was essentially what I had agreed to do anyways, since Barry had known from the beginning that my loyalty was to Johns. All Barry wanted from me was an agreement not to tell anyone other than Johns about the card, and I would live up to my bargain.

I drafted a letter letting Barry know that our professional relationship was now terminated, but I made it sound like his pressing need for a criminal attorney was the true reason behind my actions. If nothing else, this would prevent me from ethically being forced into disclosing anything I learned from here on out to Barry. I felt guilty as sin, but what had I done? It was Alex who sold out on us, and there was no way to see it coming.

By this time the sun was starting to come up, and others were starting to trickle into the office. There was way too much that had to be done right away – like making sure that Alex wasn't stealing any of our firm clients -- so my trip home for a Starbucks with Kristi and a change of clothes would have to wait. It was a decision that I would deeply regret.

Chapter 23

Brooklyn, New York
2007

As Barry Stone was taking a taxi to Manhattan to meet with the attorney to whom Chuck Evans had referred him, his cell phone rang. He answered it nonchalantly, assuming that it was Chuck calling him back for some additional instructions.

"Hello," he said, "this is Barry Stone."

"Good Morning, Mr. Stone," said a deep voice with a thick guttural accent that sounded Slavic or German. "You do not know me, but you apparently have something that interests me very much. A particular piece of cardboard, perhaps?"

"Who is this?" Stone demanded angrily. "Are you the one who had my store destroyed last night? I'll have this call traced and find out which of you Duke bastards is behind this!"

The voice on the other end remained calm and unemotional. "Mr. Stone, I can assure you that I am not affiliated with Duke University in any way. In fact, my interests run directly perpendicular to theirs." Stone noticed that the man didn't deny any involvement with the firebombing incident.

"If that's true, then how do you even know about the cards. Who told you?"

"I did not get to where I am in life by having loose lips, Mr. Stone, and I am known in certain circles to pay very handsomely for information. Thus, it seems to have a way of finding me, just as it did in this case. Please rest assured that I know about the sheet of cards and am willing to pay you handsomely for it. But I apologize; please let me introduce myself. I am Ludwig Braun, perhaps you have heard of me?"

Stone was flabbergasted. Braun was a billionaire German immigrant who had made his fortune in horse breeding and thoroughbred racing; his collection of art and antiques was known worldwide. So were his reputed ties to organized crime, although nobody had ever proven any link between him and any illegal activities. It was just a well-known fact that if Braun wanted something, he ended up with it, one way or another.

The old saying is that the population on earth with the highest rate of premature deaths is the population of people who have something that Braun wants. True, Braun's collection had mostly been purchased through estate sales – but they were estates of people who had all been perfectly healthy just a few days before their mysterious deaths. Stone could literally feel his spine tingle.

"Yes, I have heard the name," Stone replied shakily. "I apologize for my earlier outburst, Mr. Braun, it's just that I had a very long night." Stone was now convinced more than ever that it was Braun who had his store raided, but he was damn sure not going to let him know it. Stone also knew that Braun must have already opened the safe and found it empty, which was probably the only reason he was still alive. Braun needed Stone alive to lead him to the card.

"I accept your apology, Mr. Stone. And I offer my condolences to the children of the New York Foundling Orphanage, as I understand that the bank will be moving forward by the end of this week to foreclose on their precious Stratton Park."

"That's not quite accurate," Stone said, surprised at how much information Braun possessed. "The bank has agreed to extend a grace period to the orphanage until the end of the month. That should give us plenty of time to find a buyer for the Wagner cards and have the money wired to the bank to cover the note."

Braun chuckled over the phone. "I'm afraid you are mistaken, Mr. Stone. I just got off the phone with someone very powerful at the bank, and I regret to inform you that the grace period will *not* be extended. The orphanage should be receiving this bit of bad news as we speak."

Son of a bitch! Stone thought to himself. What the hell had he gotten himself into? This guy could crush him like a bug, and could probably also arrange it so that he spent the next ten years of his life in jail for arson and insurance fraud. Stone had no choice but to appear as if he would play along nicely.

"Boy, that sure makes things tough for us," Stone said sadly.

"Ah, but that's where I can step in and be of assistance, Mr. Stone. I understand that the orphanage needs seven million dollars or they lose the park. I will gladly pay you seven million dollars immediately in exchange for the entire uncut sheet. The bank will be happy, the children will be happy and best of all, I will be happy."

Stone was somewhat relieved that Braun had stated such a low price. He knew that his other potential suitors would submit higher offers, so he would have no choice but to sell it to someone other than Braun. Even selling it to the Duke Foundation would now make Stone happier than selling it to this monster.

"If I might ask, Mr. Braun, what interest do you have in baseball cards?"

"I presume you know that I am a German immigrant, Mr. Stone, who came to this country with nothing but lint in my pockets. I tended stables as a boy, and then worked my way up into the horse-trading business. Now look at me; I'm a true German success story. The same can be true of Honus Wagner.

He was the son of poor German immigrants who had three children die in infancy. He was named 'Honus' because he was so clumsy and bowlegged that the other children picked on him. He worked in the steel mills at age twelve to help support his family, where he picked up the nickname 'Dutch' from the word 'Deutsch.'

And from these humble beginnings -- not so much unlike mine -- he became one of the greatest baseball players ever to play the game: *The Flying Dutchman*. If his baseball card is going to become a national treasure, then who else should own it but a German, Mr. Stone? And I intend to be that German."

"You do understand, Mr. Braun, that I am duty bound to my client to sell the card to the entity that makes the highest offer?" Stone mentioned. "With all due respect, your offer of seven million is probably not even half of what the sheet will sell for in the end."

Braun chuckled again. "I would expect nothing less than a fair fight, Mr. Stone. If the offers that you receive from the other two potential buyers are higher than mine, then you are certainly free to sell your item to them. Perhaps I will be surprised; perhaps you will be surprised. But we will let the chips fall where they may.

Just remember that time is running out on those children, so please don't waste too much time in getting back to me to accept my generous offer."

The phone clicked as Braun hung up.

For the first time, Barry Stone realized how much he had been sweating during the call. He rolled down the window to try and cool himself off, but the July heat didn't do much to help. Even the mornings were muggy by this point in the year.

By the time Stone arrived at his new lawyer's office, he had calmed down significantly. He reminded himself that Jerry Johns and the Duke University Foundation would be bidding on the Wagner cards, so Braun's low offer would be irrelevant anyway. But the timetable had definitely been advanced by the news of the bank's decision, so Stone made plans to contact both of his other potential buyers as soon as he was finished meeting with his attorney.

Despite the ordeal that he faced with his store, the commission that he was going to make off of this same would give him a very comfortable retirement.

Chapter 24

Atlanta
2007

I worked all morning without grabbing any breakfast, so by lunchtime I was famished. Since I was still dressed in my jeans and t-shirt, I grabbed my keys and headed out to see Kristi at the sports bar. Sure, the food there was good, but seeing my new best friend in her tight little shorts was even better.

When I walked in and asked to be seated in Kristi's section, the hostess told me that Kristi hadn't shown up for work yet. Crap! I was supposed to have woken her up this morning, but with all the activity, I had completely forgotten about it. She was going to crucify me. Or worse yet, cut me off for a week.

I turned around to jog to my car and nearly trampled a middle-aged guy in a blue blazer with a buzz cut. The guy looked like Sergeant Hulka with a thick bull neck and wide shoulders -- clearly ex-military -- so thankfully he was able to dodge me or it would have been like a love bug running into a Mack truck.

"Sorry about that, my bad!" I shouted as I continued jogging to my car. I had left my cell phone at the office, so all I could do was drive home and hope that Kristi was already on her way here. Hopefully she wasn't still dead asleep, or I was the one who was going to be dead.

I covered the trip in record time and knew that I was up the creek when I saw Kristi's car still parked in the lot. Hopefully once I explained how crummy my day had been so far, Kristi would understand and forgive me. I flew into my apartment.

"Kristi, wake up!" I yelled at the top of my lungs, heading back to the bedroom. "I screwed up and you need to get up right now!"

But there was no one in the unmade bed. That wasn't like Kristi to leave the bed like that. I turned to the bathroom, expecting to see her stepping out of the shower, but the bathroom was empty as well. Now I was puzzled.

I ran back over to the window to see if her car had left, but it was still unmoved. Where the hell could she be? I guess she could have walked down the block for a Starbucks, but she wouldn't dare do that once she knew that she was late for work. I went into the kitchen to see if she had eaten anything.

My heart stopped beating when I saw a note on the kitchen table.

Oh jeez, she was so pissed at me that she'd walked out and left a "John Deere" letter for my *Dumb and Dumber* self. My inner iPod automatically switched to a new tune:

"*Don't Pull Your Love Out On Me Baby*" – Hamilton, Joe Frank and Reynolds, 1971.

Who had downloaded all of these mushy songs onto my internal library of love? Where had all my Kiss and AC/DC gone? I steadied myself for the worst as I grabbed the letter off the table and started to read, but I wasn't at all prepared for what it said:

Dear Mr. Evans:

We have your lady friend, and we intend to do her no harm. She will be released unharmed if you pay us $5,000,000 by 5:00 pm Friday. Please do whatever is needed to raise these funds. You have plenty of rich clients who should be able to loan you this amount with no problems. Start right away and we will contact you soon with further instructions. Do <u>not</u>*, however, notify anyone of this letter – especially law enforcement – or your girlfriend dies.*

Praise Allah and Osama bin Laden.

Okay, it's official, this has become the worst day of my life. "When it rains, it pours," I thought to myself, realizing how serious the situation must be if I couldn't come up with anything more Malenglish than that lame quote.

I sat down and put my head in my hands, trying to decide what the hell to do next. I couldn't call the cops for several reasons. Not only because the note forbid it, but also because the "significant other" is *always* the main suspect any time anyone disappears. I was in the same boat that Barry Stone was in!

Jesus H. Christ on a popsicle stick. How the frick am I going to come up with five million dollars by Friday? And what the hell did I do to piss off a group of Muslim terrorists? I had to do *something*; Kristi's life depended on it!

I nearly emptied my bladder in fear when the phone rang beside my head. Oh man, were they calling me already?

"Hello?" I said, trying to sound like I wasn't scared.

"I presume you found the note, Mr. Evans?" said the caller on the other end of the line. The voice sure didn't sound like an Arab speaker; he sounded almost Russian.

"Yes, I found it, but you must have the wrong man," I said. "I'd do anything to save Kristi, but I hate to tell you that my combined net savings is about $4,950,000 short of what you're asking for. Can we make some other sort of deal?"

"It's funny you should mention that," the voice said. "The note you found is merely a decoy. It does not reflect our true demands, nor does it reflect who we are. It is simply there to throw off the authorities in the event that you should choose to alert them. Of course, your girlfriend would die if you did this."

"I'm not going to tell anyone, I swear," I said desperately.

"Good, good. That's a wise decision on your part. Here is our real demand, and should you meet it, your lady friend will be released unharmed. You are not to allow your client to bid any higher than five million dollars on the Honus Wagner sheet. That's all. Nothing more is required of you. You are a smart man, so you can accomplish this task by any means you like, but you are absolutely not to mention this note or your missing girl to anyone.

If you can execute this simple task, your client will lose out on a baseball card but your lover will be released unharmed. If you fail, you may win a baseball card for your client, but you will have to live forever with the knowledge that you caused her death.

Once again, do not mention any of this to anyone – especially law enforcement. Simply convince your client to offer five million dollars so as not to raise any suspicions, but not a penny more. The girl will be released when the sale is complete."

I couldn't believe it. If I ever laid eyes on Alex again, I was going to rip his balls off! How could he have done this to Kristi and me? Hopefully the bastard was already dead. Maybe they'd killed Alex as soon as they had whatever information they needed from him. That would serve him right.

"Man, I'd heard nasty rumors about the inner workings of Big Tobacco, but you guys at Duke play dirty, don't you? All of this to protect your little university." I said, partially out of anger and partially to try and flesh out any information I could from the caller.

The low voice chuckled on the other end. "We have nothing to do with Duke. In fact, you might consider us their bitter rival at this time. Just call us the 'Tar Heels' for now."

"Well I assume you know that my client isn't the only one trying to buy the Wagners," I said. "Even if I make a low ball offer like you want, there are others like Duke's Foundation out there with far more resources than my client. I can't do jack squat to stop them from bidding the price of the card up."

"You should not concern yourself with our problems, Mr. Evans. All you need to do is keep your end of the bargain, and your girlfriend will be released unharmed once the sale is complete. Believe me, we don't want the heat that would come with a murder investigation, so we're rooting for you as hard as she is. Don't let us all down."

The phone line went dead.

I sat in silence and tried to figure this whole thing out. Obviously the people who had Kristi were the same ones that had paid off Alex and then firebombed Barry Stone's store. They were obviously some very dangerous characters, and they weren't just bluffing. Kristi's life was on the line, and I was the only one who could save her.

But hey! Look at the bright side. I didn't have to come up with any money. I didn't have to notify the cops. All I had to do was the same thing I had already done a week ago – just convince Jerry Johns that anything more than five million dollars was ridiculous and that he should never offer them a penny more. I can pull this off, right?

Chapter 25

Atlanta
2007

I still needed to eat something before I passed out, so I stuffed the fake ransom note in my pocket and sprinted to my car. I would grab something at a drive-thru and then lock myself in my office until I could straighten all of this mess out.

As I backed my car from the parking space and peeled out of the lot, I glanced to my right as I was making the turn. Son of a bitch, there was Sgt. Hulka, darting into my building! He must have been following me, and was obviously part of the group that had kidnapped Kristi. Maybe he was coming back because he had left something in my apartment, or maybe he was coming back to wipe away fingerprints. Or worse, maybe they had just decided to go ahead and kill me to get rid of the competition altogether!

Either way, I'm now a man on the run with no place to hide. I'm too scared to go back to my apartment, so I guess I'll be sleeping at my office for a while. Thankfully I've got a few outfits in my closet there, or I'll start to look like a homeless person with only one set of clothes.

I got a Subway and wolfed it down on my way back to work. If I could just get Jerry Johns to agree that buying the card was not in his best interest, then all of my problems would be solved. Who would ever know why I had given him that advice?

No sooner had I sat down then Angie buzzed me to let me know that Barry Stone was holding on line five and had already called six times in the past thirty minutes. Obviously something was eating him up. Hopefully he hadn't already been arrested.

"Hey Barry," I said, trying to get myself back in a normal frame of mind, and being extremely careful not to accidentally spill the beans about Kristi's kidnapping in any way. "How'd your meeting with the attorney go?"

"Fine, thanks. I appreciate the help with that, Chuck, I really do," Stone said sincerely. "In fact, I've been thinking, and I think I could convince Dr. Marinolli to sell your client the uncut sheet for something well under market value, just to make sure the deal gets done sooner rather than later. I'm thinking something in the twelve million dollar range.

That's only two million apiece for each Wagner, which as you know is well below the market price. I've been offered seven million for the sheet, but that's way too low and I'm compelled to sell it to the highest bidder. Hopefully you've talked to your client and he's ready to pull the trigger?"

"Well," I said slowly, "we may have a problem. I've discussed this with the Big Stick until I was blue in the face, and I can't convince him to pay anything more than five million for it. If you can get seven for it, then I'm happy for you and your client, but it's out of our range."

On the other end of the phone line, Barry Stone was at his wits end. This was the guy whose client wanted to pay "whatever it took" to buy a single T-206 Wagner just a short time ago, and now he was getting cheap when a *six-pack* of Wagners was available? What was going on? Would he be forced to sell it for less than half of its value to Ludwig Braun and give up hundreds of thousands of dollars in commissions?

"I don't understand, Chuck," Stone pleaded. "I thought you had agreed that this item was worth close to twenty million, and now you can only get your client to offer *five* for it? Am I missing something?"

No, Chuck thought to himself, *I'm* missing something – namely the first girl I think I've ever really loved. It would be so much easier if he could confide in Barry, but he just couldn't take the risk.

"No, Barry, I think you're probably right in your appraisal," I agreed, "but I think the Stickman is just used to doing things his way or the highway. For whatever reason he is set on his price, so now it's just a matter of principle for him. Remember, this is a guy who really can look at Honus Wagner and say 'I'm better at this game than he was.' So maybe Jerry is just jealous that nobody is offering to pay this kind of money for *his* card."

"I'm just sorry to hear all of this, Chuck. I was really hoping we could make this deal work. You know this opportunity will never come again, right?"

"Yeah, Barry, I know," I said.

"Just do me a favor," Stone begged. "Just keep talking to your client and I'll keep talking to mine. Maybe something will happen before the deadline that changes things."

I agreed to keep an open dialogue with Barry and bid him farewell. I rocked back in my chair and closed my eyes in thought. Had I followed the instructions properly? Would the news get back to Sgt. Hulka so that was I safe to return home? How could I let the kidnappers know that I had done my job?

Screw it, if Stone was telling the truth and someone – I assume Duke – has already offered him seven million dollars for the thing, then the kidnappers now have other problems to deal with. They may have knocked me out of the running, but what good is it going to do them when Duke will spend whatever it takes to get the card from Stone?

And damn it, how will the kidnappers know that it isn't *me* that's driving up the price? If they think I'm doing it, then I'll never see Kristi again. I couldn't live with myself if that happens. I wish I had some way of contacting the kidnappers.

Wait a second. Maybe I do! As much I want to cut off his balls right now, at least Alex could serve as a conduit for information from me to the kidnappers. I still had his personal e-mail address on my computer, so I sent him a terse note that said:

Alex: Please let them know that I've done my part of the bargain. I'll find a way to forgive you if you can help Kristi now. - Chuck

It was generic enough that it could never be understood by someone who wasn't aware of the situation, but it was specific enough to get the job done. Hopefully that turncoat Alex will read his e-mail and help us…if he isn't already dead or drinking rum on a tropical island by now.

Chapter 26

Atlanta
2007

Kristi had been blindfolded with duct tape wrapped firmly around her head, both over and under her ponytail. There was no way she could get it off without a great deal of effort, but she didn't even bother to try since they had her under constant surveillance the entire time anyway. At least they had not tied her up or gagged her. She was free to move her limbs, and she had been talking to her captors as often as possible in hopes of gathering clues to their location or identity.

She had left Chuck's apartment and was just about to get into her car when she had noticed a delivery van pulling into the parking lot behind her. It was from a florist shop that she was unfamiliar with, but the thought of someone getting flowers made her happy for whoever the lucky person was.

"Ma'am, I have a delivery for someone from a Chuck Evans, but I can't read his writing to get the name right," said the driver through his open window as he stopped the van right behind her car and hopped out. "Are you the lady that Chuck Evans would be sending flowers to?"

Wow! She had missed Chuck's company this morning as she had woken up in bed alone, but she knew that he had received an important call very early that morning from someone about a fire, so she completely understood why he had bolted to the office instead of sticking around for one of her gourmet breakfasts of Fruity Pebbles and Brown Sugar Cinnamon Pop-Tarts. Who said modern women were lacking in the culinary arts?

"I guess they're for me – or at least they'd better be. I'm his girlfriend. Does it maybe say 'Kristi' on the card?"

"Yeah, that's it, you're a lucky lady," said the driver as he made his way around the rear of the enclosed windowless van. "If you will just come back here and sign for this, I'll give it to you and be on my way. It's a really big one."

Kristi's emotions were really pumping now, as she hadn't received flowers from a boyfriend in years. True, she gave off the impression to most boyfriends that she would prefer an Adam Sandler DVD over flowers (who wouldn't?), but this was definitely a nice change of pace.

As the driver opened one of the rear side-by-side doors, he gestured for Kristi to look inside. "Look at the size of that thing in there!"

As Kristi went to crane her neck around the open door and see what he was pointing at, she suddenly felt the driver clamp his hand over her mouth from behind and shove her forward, into the arms of another man who was wearing a ski mask. The masked man grabbed her and yanked her into the van as the other man slammed the door before she even had time to scream. The interior of the van was lit, and the masked man showed her his pistol as she lay still in a daze on the mattress on the floor.

"Look," he said roughly, "we don't want no trouble with you. If everyone cooperates, you'll be free in a few days. Understand?"

Kristi nodded and prayed that he was telling the truth.

He continued giving her instructions. "Here's the drill. I'm going to blindfold you so that you don't know where we're taking you, but once we're there, you will be made as comfortable as possible. Like I said, we want to treat you nice so that once you're set free, you appreciate our hospitality and don't try to send the Feds after us. Of course, if you did, we would know who had done it and we would just find you again and kill you without batting an eye that time."

Kristi could tell this man was not kidding. He had killed before, and had probably even enjoyed it. She knew that she had to be on her best behavior and do her best to get on his good side.

"Okay, I get the picture," Kristi said, as she allowed the man to wrap the duct tape around her head. "I'm not going to try and be a hero or anything like that."

"That's good," said the man as he finished the blindfolding job. "We'll leave that up to your boyfriend. If he can follow some simple instructions, you'll be back in his arms in no time. Then maybe you'll owe *him* some flowers," the man snickered.

Kristi realized then that the van still hadn't moved from where it had been parked. Maybe someone had spotted her abduction and was fighting with the driver? But the parking lot had been virtually empty when she left the building, since all of the cars had left for work many hours ago. Her car had been the only one on that whole side of the building.

Just then she heard a loud noise that startled her and caused her insides to turn. She had never realized how scary it would be in the dark with no ability to open her eyes or turn on some lights. Every minute was tense because unseen harm could be only a second or an inch away. She finally exhaled when she realized it was just the driver's door slamming as he had gotten back in the van.

"Relax," the man in the rear said to her as the driver put the van in gear and started driving. "If I was going to shoot you, it wouldn't be in here. Too loud and too messy. In here, if you act up, I would just strangle you with my bare hands. But like I said, my orders are to treat you like a queen – so don't make me have to behead the queen, okay?"

Kristi nodded eagerly, hoping he was watching.

"Did you put the note where it would be found easily?" the man in the rear asked the driver.

"Sure did, right on the kitchen table. It's the only thing there so nobody can miss it, and I put a cup on it to make sure it didn't blow off or something. Hey lady, I wasn't kidding about having something big for you back there, was I?" he shouted, laughing at his own joke.

Kristi sat silent for a while, realizing that the ride to wherever they were going was a long one once she felt the van accelerate and get into what felt like highway driving.

"I don't get it," Kristi finally pleaded. "Who are you guys and what are you kidnapping *me* for? Are you *sure* you've got the right person? My parents are both teachers up in Tennessee; they don't have any money for a ransom or anything."

"Don't worry, honey, you're the right person all right. In fact, your parents aren't even going to know you're missing if we can get this thing done and cut you loose in a few days. I know *we* certainly aren't going to tell them. Your boyfriend isn't supposed to either. If he wants you back alive, he'll be smart enough to just make up an excuse and cover for you if anyone comes looking."

"In the meantime," the man sitting next to her in the rear of the van continued," you can just call me 'Gale' and my brother up front there is 'Evelle.' If you haven't figured it out by now, we're the Snopes brothers, and we're using *code* names."

Kristi couldn't believe that she could actually laugh under these trying circumstances, but she really couldn't help herself. She knew that bonding with these guys would improve her chances of survival, and she never imagined she'd be living out a scene from *Raising Arizona* herself.

"Good one," Kristi said with a smile that she hoped they could see. "But since my dad doesn't own a furniture store in Arizona called 'Unpainted Huffhines', I don't see what you guys want with little old Nathan Jr. here."

The driver burst out into laughter. "How 'bout that, Gale. We finally found a girl who would enjoy watching all of our guy movies with us back at the base, but we can't take her blindfold off. Sucks, huh?"

"Suh-suh-suh-suh...?" the man in the rear answered his Judge Smails voice, as if on cue.

"Yeah, that's right. Sucks!" replied the driver, again laughing uncontrollably at his *Caddyshack* moment.

Kristi offered a Judge Smails impression of her own. "Kidnapping is illegal at Bushwood...and I *never* slice."

That one got both of them laughing.

"Sweetheart, we aren't kidnapping you," the driver said over his shoulder, "we're just entertaining you for a few days while your boyfriend finishes up a business deal with a friend of ours. So you just sit back and enjoy the ride."

That has been several hours ago, before the van had finally stopped at some remote location where Kristi had been unloaded and taken inside. She could hear big metal sliding doors being opened and closed, so it sounded like they were in an abandoned warehouse somewhere. She was led into an air conditioned office and made to sit on a couch.

"Okay, miss, here's the program," the man who had been in the rear of the van said to her. "I know you can't see, but you need to trust me when I tell you that there is going to be someone with a gun watching you at all times. Even if he's not in the room here with you, he'll be watching you on the video monitor. There's nothing in this room you can use as a weapon, but don't bother trying to find one anyway since we'd see you doing it and we wouldn't like it.

If you can just sit there on the couch like a good girl, we'll play some movies and let you at least listen to them. We'll feed you often, and we'll let you use the restroom over there whenever you let us know you need to. There's no windows here anyway, so you aren't going anywhere even if you are the second-coming of *MacGyver*. You got all that? Are we cool-de-la?

"Yeah, we're cool-de-la," Kristi answered. "*I'm your Caucasian*. Best episode ever, if you ask me."

"I agree," Gale snapped, "but Evelle over there thinks the one with Barry and the hooker in the carpool lane to the Dodgers' game is the funniest."

"It is!" Evelle said defensively. "When Barry's too cheap to buy her a hot dog and she says '*I'm gonna pull a titty out!* --that's unbeatable. And how about Barry trying to figure out the difference between *chronic* and *schwag* when he's buying pot for his dad's glaucoma? Had me rolling on the floor!"

Kristi found it hard to believe that these two clowns were the brains behind any mastermind criminal activity. She knew they were only the hired muscle, which meant that they would kill her in an instant if ordered to do so by whoever was paying the bill. Who was their boss, and what business did he have with Chuck that was so damned important? She had to find out, just in case she did find a way to survive this ordeal.

"I'm going to be a model citizen, I promise," Kristi said again, "but can you give me some hope of when I might get out of here? Are you sure my boyfriend knows what he has to do to get me back home?"

"Actually, missy, it's what he *isn't* supposed to do that's the key to your freedom," the driver who called himself Evelle said. "The guy probably hasn't bought baseball cards in thirty years, so if he can just go another few days without buying any more, you'll be back home before anyone's even started looking for you."

Good Lord! *That's* what this was all about? Her life now in hung in the balance because of a stupid piece of cardboard? Kristi knew how excited Chuck had been about getting the card for his most important client, Jerry Johns, so now she started to really worry even more than before.

How much *do* I really mean to Chuck? she wondered. How sure was she that he wouldn't just close the deal for his client that would make him famous on national television and let her die in the process? If he did it, nobody but Chuck and these kidnappers would ever really know what had happened to her, and none of them would want anybody to know. She'd just become another face on the side of a milk carton.

The only song that she could hear playing over and over in her head was another oldie from the jukebox where she worked:

"I Need a Hero / I'm Holding Out For a Hero" –
Bonnie Tyler, 1984

Chapter 27

Brooklyn
2007

"You're the best, Dr. Joe!" Roland exclaimed as he sat up on the edge of Joe Marinolli's hospital bed, leaning over to hug Joe as best he could with his undersized arms. Joe patted him on the back with his free arm that wasn't hooked up to an IV tube and marveled at how strong Ro's appendages were for their tiny size.

"Hey, careful there, Ro," Joe said with a laugh, able to talk now that his breathing tube was removed. "You're so strong you might squeeze the life right out of me!"

Ro went pale and nearly fell off the bed as he reeled back in horror.

"Oh no, I'm just kidding!" Joe said quickly. "I guess that wasn't a good choice of words!"

"All the kids back home are so excited about you trying to save our baseball field, Dr. Joe," Ro said eagerly after he had recovered from his fright. "You're our hero, even if it doesn't work. Everyone knows you're trying. We're even gathering up all of our baseball cards to help!"

"That's great, Roland," Barry Stone said with a smile as he stood on the other side of Joe's bed. "I'll be sure to look through those too and see if you guys come up with any hidden gems."

"Hey, I got a Derek Jeter foil insert card the other day!" Ro piped up. "Somebody will want that for sure! He's better than that Homer guy, or Hocus, or whatever his name is that Dr. Joe is selling!"

"Well let's hope you're right, Roland," Tom Bennett said with a laugh from his chair at the end of the bed. "We need all the money we can get."

Bennett turned to Stone. "The deadline for payment's now less than forty-eight hours away, Barry. What's the deal with your Atlanta connection bailing out?"

"I really don't have any explanation for it," Stone said, "other than cold feet."

"But I thought Jerry Johns wanted to buy the sheet of cards *and* come visit the children at the orphanage for a promotional appearance. That type of publicity would do wonders for our future fundraising and capital campaigns," Bennett said. "I'm thinking we might be better off selling it for five million to Johns and letting the park go. These types of opportunities don't come often. It would probably *cost* us a million dollars to get someone like him to do a public service announcement for us anyways."

"No way, Tom," Joe said firmly. "I'm not selling it for anything less than what it's worth. This is my and my father's one and only opportunity to leave a lasting legacy with the orphanage, so I want to get everything we can for the cards. And there is *no way* I'm letting the kids lose their park. Have you been out to watch any of their baseball games? I've never seen any group of people have so much fun.

For those brief moments, they completely forget any of the sadness or sorrow that comes with not having parents. When they're at that park, they're no different than any other kids in America. Without the park, they'll be stuck at the orphanage all day every day; they'll be cooped up like chickens and depression will set in."

"Fine," Tom said, "it's your item and you can certainly do what you want with it. What do you think, Barry, you're the one who appraised the sheet at fifteen million or so. Think the price is too high, and maybe that's why Johns and his crew are balking? Think they're just negotiating with us?"

"No, I don't get that feeling," Stone said. "I made it clear to Chuck Evans that we already had a buyer willing to pay seven million for it, so unless he thinks I'm flat out bluffing, he knows that his bid is way too low. Maybe he'll call me back at some point and have a change of heart, but I would be surprised based on what I heard from Chuck."

"Okay, so where does that leave us?" Joe asked.

"We have another big time buyer who is willing to pay seven million for it," Stone advised them, "which is a terrible deal for us because it leaves as much as maybe ten million dollars on the table."

"But it lets us pay off the bank and keep Stratton Park," Bennett piped in.

"That's true," Stone admitted.

"And who is this buyer?" Joe asked.

"I'm sure you've heard of Ludwig Braun, the thoroughbred horsing magnate? He's done his homework and knows exactly how much you owe the bank," Stone said to

Bennett, "so it's no coincidence that his offer is right in line with that amount. It's a typical hardball play on his part. It's how the rich get richer – off other people's misfortunes."

"Ludwig Braun, the German mobster?" Joe asked with a raised voice. *"He's* the one who wants these cards? Well he'll have to get them over my dead body!"

"First of all, don't even joke like that, Joe," Stone warned him. "With a guy like Braun and all of his connections, the likelihood of that happening is a lot higher than you think."

"I'm not joking, Barry," Joe said sternly. "There's no way in hell that I'll let Braun buy the cards."

"Why not?" asked Barry.

"Because he's a German," Joe said, fighting back tears. "Don't you get it? Don't you know why I never met my father? Joe's voice was getting louder, and his face was turning red. "Don't you know why my mother was a widow for pretty much her entire adult life? The Germans killed my father in World War One, and if wasn't for this damned polio of mine, I would have signed up for World War Two and killed as many of them as possible.

If there is one thing I know my dad would want more than saving Stratton Park, it's screwing a German – especially one as crooked and heavy-handed as Ludwig Braun!"

"Okay, Joe, okay. Don't get so worked up," Bennett said as he poured Joe a glass of water from his bedside pitcher. "I'm sure Barry can handle this in a diplomatic way, right Barry?"

Stone nodded. "I'm not going to do *anything* without your full permission, Joe, so just forget I even mentioned Braun. Like I said, his offer is nowhere near what the whole sheet's is worth. In fact, I don't think we're going to have anything to worry about in a few hours."

"Why's that?" Bennett asked.

"Because I'm waiting to hear back from the Duke University people," Stone said, "and they think it's going to take fifteen million *at least* to get the piece. I've told them about the new deadline, so my guess is that they'll come in way above that just to make sure they get the cards and no one else does."

"But they'll destroy the cards, won't they," Joe asked sadly.

"I have no way of knowing for sure," Stone said, "but if I had to guess, I would say yes. I know that's not what you want, Joe, but we can take as many photographs and digital images of the sheet as we want before we sell it. Let them destroy the originals, but we'll still have pictures of it to display at the orphanage along with a plaque honoring the Marinolli family for their munificence and generosity. Right, Tom?"

"Oh absolutely!" Bennett exclaimed, excited once again about the prospect of the orphanage gaining a donation in excess of fifteen million dollars. "I'll carve the damned plaque myself if I have to!"

"And just so you know," Stone continued, "I've spoken with the National Baseball Hall of Fame in Cooperstown, and they're also willing to put up a display with one of our photographs of the uncut sheet and a placard mentioning the Marinolli family's history with it."

"Oh my God," Joe gasped, "are you serious?"

"I guess this isn't the right time or place for me to say 'as a heart attack,' huh?" Stone said sheepishly with a grin on his face.

"I can't believe it! My father is going to have his name in the Baseball Hall of Fame! Right there with the heroes of his childhood! Great sakes alive, I know he's up in heaven celebrating with my mom right now about this one!"

Joe got quiet for a minute and then turned to Stone. "Barry, is Frank Bowerman in the Hall of Fame?"

"No, he was pretty much just a journeyman who never really starred anywhere. Did you ever figure out why your father had a fascination with him?"

"No, I'll probably never know the answer to that one," Joe said sadly. I'm guessing it had something to do with his childhood in New York around that 1909 period. It may have even been something that he got from *his* father before he died of Typhoid Fever back near the turn of the century."

"Well, if that's true," Stone said cheerfully, "then your grandfather and Frank Bowerman are right there partying with your mom and dad – because Frank Bowerman's finally going into the Hall of Fame when this sheet goes on display! In fact, he'll be right there front and center, between Honus Wagner and Cy Young. Holy cow, what great company to have for eternity!"

They all laughed heartily.

"Okay, Barry," Joe said. "You've convinced me. You go work your magic on the guys from Duke and get them to pay us twenty million. If I can get *that* much for the orphanage, then they can roll up the sheet and smoke it for all I care!"

Chapter 28

Atlanta
2007

I kept checking my e-mail, but I had still not received a response from Alex. I guess I was stupid to expect one, but I was praying that he had read mine to him and was passing the word to Sgt. Hulka and his band of kidnappers that I had done my part of the deal. I hadn't heard Hulka speak when I'd almost trampled him coming out of Kristi's work, but he sure looked exactly like I thought the person who had called me would look. Big Slavic looking guy with wide features. Maybe Russian, maybe German?

What am I doing? The girl I love has been kidnapped by a group of killers over a freakin' baseball card, and I'm working *with* the criminals to help keep it a secret instead of calling the FBI and getting them involved? I'm so screwed. If she gets out alive, she'll know that I never called law enforcement. Hopefully she'll understand that it was because I wanted her to live so bad; hopefully she won't look at it another way and decide to turn me in as a accomplice.

And the hardest thing is sitting here at the office trying to act normal so that nobody finds out about the whole mess. Just a few minutes ago, Jim came in with a wonderfully juicy bit of Malenglish minutia, and I had to play along while my mind was a million miles away.

"*Undercover Angel*?" Jim asked, holding a sheet in his hand that obviously held the answer fresh off the internet.

"I don't know, who?" I had replied absentmindedly, creating a slight breach of Malenglish etiquette.

You were never supposed to skip straight to the answer. Proper manners require one to exhaust all efforts before learning the solution to the puzzle. It is the "thrill of the hunt" that makes the whole dialogue worthwhile. In other words, the resolution of the problem *ends* the conversation and forces us males to then make *more* conversation. Who wants to do that if you don't have to?

Jim looked at me like I had called him a bad name. "Damn, man, who put a turd in your sandwich?" he asked.

"I'm sorry, man, I've just had a bad day," I muttered.

"Are things okay with Kristi?" he asked.

"What do you mean?" I asked urgently, my voice raising. "Who told you? Have you been talking to Alex or something?" I walked around behind him and slammed the door shut.

"Chuck, is everything all right?" Jim asked with concern. "I don't know what the hell you're talking about, but you know that Alex is the last motherscratcher I ever want to see again. That son of a bitch has a chance to stay here and help me make partner, and the dickhead hauls ass in the middle of the night somewhere else at the drop of a dollar. I was just wondering if you and Kristi had been in a fight or something."

"Jeez, I'm sorry," I said, sitting back down in relief. "I'm just so messed up by this Alex crap that I can't think straight either. We still don't know whether or not he stole any of our clients from us. So far nobody has defected, but they may just be biding their time. He'll have to surface at some point, and we'll get our chance to give him a piece of our mind then."

But in the back of my mind, I still couldn't shake the image of Alex lying dead somewhere after having been bled for information that he thought was going to make him rich.

"Well, I'll just tell you the answer anyway. *Undercover Angel* was Alan O'Day."

"I would have never known that one," I confessed. Now it was my turn to honor the Malenglish tradition of exchanging gifts. I couldn't just let him give me something without giving him something back.

"Okay, this one is sports and music combined," I said. "Who sang the song that you hear sports fan singing near the end of a game when their team is killing the other team – '*Na na na na...hey hey hey, good bye*'?"

"That was a real song?" Jim asked, showing his youth.

"Yep, from 1969."

"Considering that was about thirteen years before I was born, I don't feel so bad not knowing the answer," Jim said, "so I'll guess Bryan Adams."

"Bryan Adams? He doesn't sound anything like that, and he came around about a decade or so later."

"Yeah," Jim said with a smile as he turned around to leave, "but he bought his first real six string at the five and dime in 1969."

"Clever," I said with a grin. "but the correct answer is Steam."

"Steam, huh? Never heard of 'em."

"How about that? Both Steam *and* Alan O'Day just gained one new fan each. That probably makes a dozen total for them combined," I chuckled as Jim left the room.

Just as I was on the verge of sending another desperation e-mail to Alex, the receptionist buzzed me on the intercom.

"Call for you on line four," she said quickly before hanging up.

When Angie's out of the office, my calls come through the front desk, but the girl out there is so busy scrambling for different lines that she never has time to ask who's calling.

Crap, were the kidnappers calling me here? Dang, where's that miniature recorder that I use for dictation? I know it's around here somewhere. If I can record this call, I can at least have *some* proof that I'm not the one responsible for Kristi's disappearance. I found the machine and started recording.

"Hello, Chuck Evans. How may I help you?"

"Hey Chuck, it's Barry Stone. You got a minute?"

"Honestly, I don't, Barry. I'm knee deep in a some future fertilizer here, if you know what I mean."

"Okay, then I'll get right to the point," said Barry. "I'm begging you to *please* talk to your client again and see if he will buy this sheet of cards for seven million. It's an absolute steal and I should be shot for even considering it, but the consignor, Dr. Marinolli, is pressed to sell ASAP and refuses to sell it to the only buyer who has already offered seven million."

"Why? That doesn't make any sense," I mentioned.

"It does to him. That potential buyer is a well-known German immigrant up here who has become very wealthy and could afford to pay ten times that amount, but he is playing hardball and won't go any higher. But his offer's irrelevant, because Dr. Marinolli won't sell it to a German. He lost his father in World War One to a German sniper, and he's never forgiven them."

"So what about the tobacco estate; the Duke Trust? I know you're pissed off at them for thinking that they robbed your store, but you really don't have any hard proof that it was them. Don't you owe it to your consignor to get them in the bidding? Heck, they'll pay *way* more than seven million for this whole sheet of Wagners. They would solve all your problems."

Stone knew that it was Ludwig Braun's men who firebombed his store and not anyone associated with Duke, but he didn't dare share this with anyone. The last thing he wanted was to be in a war with Braun even *after* this particular sale had taken place. He decided to stretch the truth.

"Chuck, I know it sounds easy, but I'll never forgive the Duke group for what they did to my business. I've discussed it with my consignor, and he agrees. The German and Duke University are *both* ineligible buyers for this item in our mind. Maybe we're crazy, but we think it's the right thing to do morally. That's why *your client* is so important to us now and why he could get a great deal on an incredibly rare and important piece of American history."

"But remember," Stone continued, adding some puffery purely for negotiation purposes, "there are several other people I am talking to about this card, and I expect good strong offers from them soon. You need to act *now* if your client wants the sheet."

"Okay Barry, I'll do my best on the sale and get back to you shortly. I know it's getting down to 'fish or cut bait' time," I said as I hung up, knowing in my mind that there was no way possible I could increase our bid and not end up killing Kristi at the same time.

I was losing hundreds of thousands of dollars in fees on this, not to mention the opportunity to be on every national network and in every national newspaper with the Big Stick showing off his new card. My internal iPod had the perfect tune for this one:

"The Things We Do For Love" – 10cc, 1976.

If Barry Stone had only told me the truth at that moment, the two of us would probably have pieced it all together. If he had told me that it had been Braun who torched his store and not someone affiliated with Duke, I would have realized that it was probably Braun who had kidnapped Kristi.

Or, more importantly, if Barry had told me that he had just finished speaking with the President of the Duke Foundation before calling me and that Duke was *not bidding at all* on the card for some unknown reason, then I might have seen the big picture a little clearer.

And if Barry had not mentioned all of his other potential buyers, I would have known that Braun was the only person still bidding on the card. That alone would have convinced me that Braun was behind Kristi's disappearance.

But as it was, only Stone knew that Duke had completely bailed out of the bidding, and I couldn't blame him later for not sharing this knowledge since everything is fair in sales negotiations of this magnitude.

And since the Braun name didn't ring a bell with me, I had no idea that he was "connected" enough to pull off a kidnapping. I assumed he was just another legitimate businessman. He was out of my mind as soon as Barry quit talking about him, because the only person I feared right now was the big Russian-looking guy with the crew cut that I had dubbed "Sgt. Hulka" and who was probably still waiting for me at my apartment with a gun or something worse.

In the end, saving Kristi was my only objective, so I had no choice. I would call Barry back tomorrow and once again bid only five million dollars just as I had been instructed to do by the kidnappers. I'd let Barry figure out what to do about his client's deadline for saving the park.

Oh crap! An alarm started screaming in my head, sounding like a submarine starting to dive. I just had a terrible thought!

Barry just told me that they aren't going to sell the sheet to the German guy or to Duke. So what if they don't get any more bids and decided to sell to the highest bidder? Then *I* end up winning the freakin' thing! Talk about a cluster pluck!

If I won the card, it would be like me giving the middle finger to the kidnappers, or thumbing my nose at them. They would be so pissed off that Kristi would surely suffer some terrible torture before being mercifully snuffed out!

And even worse, it would absolutely cement *me* as the primary number one suspect in her disappearance. It's bad enough that I'm the "significant other," but if it ever looks to anyone like I profited from her disappearance, I was looking at the death penalty for sure. Executing a dirty lawyer would be such a big event down here in Georgia, they'd probably sell tickets and let everyone watch me get killed right there during intermission of the next monster truck show.

But hold on. Wasn't Kristi kidnapped so that whoever did it could outbid me and buy the card? If so, then that person would be calling Barry Stone soon and placing a bid slightly higher than five million, right? They were just holding out until the end to make sure it would still be in their price range, right?

Or maybe the whole thing was an elaborate ruse? Maybe I *am* supposed to win the card for five million? Who the heck would benefit from that? The bank in New York would!

They wanted Stratton Park for themselves, so they are hoping that the orphanage will come up short by tomorrow and miss the payment deadline. If the card only sells for five million, the orphanage will still survive, but they'll just lose their park. And since the orphanage owes the bank seven million dollars, the five million they get from the sale is going to go straight back to the bank anyway!

Damn, this is so confusing! Am I supposed to win the card or not? I *had* to get in touch with the kidnappers! My only choice again was to e-mail that asshole Alex and pray that he still had some shred of decency left in him. Hopefully he would pass my message on to his new puppeteer.

Alex: I just want Kristi back and alive. I offered $5 mil for the card, but am afraid I may win at that price. Please advise ASAP if this is good or bad. I'll do whatever I'm told, but the sale date is tomorrow so please hurry. - Chuck

Chapter 29

Somewhere near Savannah
2007

Kristi couldn't believe how disoriented she had become without her vision. Not only could she not see what time it was, she had no idea whether it was day or night. And every time she fell asleep and awoke, she had no idea if she had been asleep for eight minutes or eight hours. They didn't feed her meals at any regular interval so she couldn't use that to judge what time it might be, nor did they serve breakfast or lunch or dinner. It was all the same; instant food that they would just pop in the microwave any time she requested it. She simply had no idea how long she had been there by now.

As she was lying on the couch feigning sleep, Kristi heard the guard in her room walk rapidly across the concrete floor and open the door. It sounded as if he headed out into the warehouse and left the door open, because Kristi could now hear a commotion from outside her room somewhere.

"I don't know who you think you're messing with, but my daddy won't give you a damn penny for me!" she heard a young female shout. "He hasn't given me the time of day for fifteen years, so I don't know why you think he'll want me back!"

"Just let us worry about that, okay missy?" said a voice that she recognized as the driver from her van. "Like we told you, we don't run the show here, and we don't make the rules. We just do as we're told. Apparently somebody thinks you're worth something, so just cooperate and you'll be home in no time."

"Home? You think I want to go *home*? Ha! I'll make a deal with you, old man. Take me to Beverly Hills and drop me off there where my old man can't find me, and I'll pay you something extra on top of what you're asking him for!"

That was the last thing Kristi heard as the door to another office down the hall slammed shut. Apparently they had taken the girl in there.

Jeez! Kristi thought to herself. These guys are running a kidnapping convenience store here! She had thought that she was the only one there, but now she was worried that the place was *full* of young girls. Could this be a sex slave ring? Maybe they really didn't have any intentions of ever letting her go? Maybe that's why they were treating her so nice, because they needed her to be in good condition when they sold her?

For once, a quick painless death almost seemed like the best alternative.

Chapter 30

Atlanta
2007

"*Fooled Around and Fell In Love*" – Elvin Bishop, 1976.

I'd just asked myself how the heck I'd gotten into this whole damn mess, and before I could even consider my rhetorical question, the next song in my iTunes library had started playing the answer for me out loud. True, I hadn't been through a million girls like the guy in the song, but falling in love after all these years was like jumping out of an airplane for the first time; my stomach had been doing somersaults ever since.

"Free Fallin' " – Tom Petty, 1989.

Angie buzzed in, "it's Jerry Johns on line two, and he doesn't sound happy."

Okay, now my stomach feels like I pulled the ripcord and my parachute didn't open. Dang it! I thought I had all my bases covered, and I wasn't planning on talking to Johns again until *after* the card had sold. I'd conveniently forgotten to tell him that I wasn't going to follow through on his order to pay whatever it took to buy the sheet of Wagner cards. My plan was to just let someone else buy the stupid thing for a ton of money and then tell him afterwards that I had quit bidding because of authenticity questions about the card or some other excuse.

I assumed he would never know the difference, so why would he be upset with me now? I decided to tackle this head on, like a man.

"Can you please take a message for me, Angie?" I said over the intercom. "Just tell him I'm on another call and will get back to him as soon as I get some news on his item."

I hung up and stared at my phone, noticing with dread that the indicator light for line two was still flashing.

I was having an Ed Rooney moment.

"He said he'll hold for as long as it takes," Angie said as she came back on the line, "and he said to tell you that he knows you only bid five million, and he wants to talk about why you're being so cheap all of a sudden."

How the hell did he know? Okay, no problem, I could handle this.

I picked up the phone and put it to my ear.

"Hey, Stick, how's it going?" I asked nonchalantly.

"It's going fine right now, but if tomorrow comes and goes without me getting those damn cards, I'm gonna get on a plane to Africa and go pick up your daddy myself so that I can get him back over here and we can *both* fire your ass!"

Okay, maybe I couldn't handle this.

"Calm down, big man, calm down," I said. "These sales don't even get started until the very end. It's just like on eBay these days. Nobody bids until there's only five seconds left so that nobody else can see their bid and have time to outbid them. It's called 'sniping' and everybody does it. Heck, our five million dollar offer is currently in first place, so if they sold the card today, it would be yours."

"So you're just bluffing to see if we can get everyone else to show their hands, huh?" Johns asked.

"Yep," I replied. "I just sort of lollygagged into this auction, and then I'm going to act disinterested and lollygag every time they call – all the way up until the very end. You know what that makes us, Jerry?"

"Lollygaggers?"

"Lollygaggers!"

"Great movie. You know, Chuck, I played in the minor leagues for a little bit, and that's a pretty accurate description of what it's like, man. Run down stadiums and long bus rides to nowhere. I had a lot of managers just like that guy; they would yell about everything."

"Well you know what other famous role that guy who played the manager was in, don't you?" I asked.

"No, not off the top of my head," Johns said.

"His name's Trey Wilson, and he also played Nathan Arizona."

"Are you kidding me?" Johns exclaimed.

"I'm crapping you negative!" I replied. "But tell me this, Jerry. How did you know that I had only offered five million? Did you call here and talk to Jim or Angie?"

"Naw, I just got a package of junk Fed Ex'd to me today from the guy selling the thing. Barry Stone, that's the guy, right? He sent a brochure with pictures of the thing, along with an article talking about it and some certificates showing that it's real. He had it all shipped to the equipment manager here at the stadium, and he brought it to me just a few minutes ago."

"Yeah, Barry Stone, that's who I'm dealing with. He sent stuff directly to you, huh?"

I guess I was angry at Barry for not dealing directly with me, but legally he was free to contact Jerry Johns directly just like he could anyone else in America. And shoot, I was the one jilting Barry by pulling out of the bidding unannounced, so I guess he was only doing what any good seller would do for his consignor: trying to drum up interest.

"What'd it say specifically," I asked.

"It said that the sheet was appraised at more than fifteen million, and it reminded me that the sale had to be finalized by tomorrow afternoon. Then it mentioned that my final bid was only five million dollars, and that's what set me through the roof. I may not have a college degree, but even I can figure out that we should be offering more than five if the thing's really worth fifteen."

"And we will, Jerry, we will," I assured him. "You just go back to playing ball, and the next time we talk it will be to start scheduling you for some promotional photographs and interviews. You'll get the card, *and* you'll look like a hero for saving that park for kids at the orphanage."

"I'll be sure to remove my grill for that," Johns laughed. "I know how jealous you honkies get when I flash those diamonds and gold!"

"And you can lose the fake ghetto slang, too, while you're at it," I said laughing. "You seem to forget that I've heard you talk normal. All that reading you did on those bus rides you talked about; your damn vocabulary's more expansive than mine!"

"I concur wholeheartedly," Johns quipped in a fake British accent. "But alas, I am obliged to resort to the modern African-American vernacular in order to form a bond with my aficionados. Please forgive me for my usage of colloquial speech at any occasion from this day hence."

"On second thought," I said, "stick with the home boy rap. You play baseball, not cricket. You start talking like that and people are going to think Louis Winthorpe got back inside Billy Ray Washington's body."

The Stickman laughed. "Looking good, Billy Ray!"

"Feeling good, Winthorpe!"

"Okay, Chuck, I trust you. Go buy that thing for the best price you can, and I look forward to hearing about it tomorrow night after my game. But don't even bother calling if you don't win, because I'll be busy agent shopping."

"*Well...isn't that special*?" I though to myself in my best Church Lady Chuck as the call ended.

I grabbed a Cherry Coke Zero from the mini-fridge and took a big swig. Dang, that tasted just like a cherry coke. How would we ever really know whether it wasn't just the same liquid in a different bottle? Who checks up on that stuff?

But more importantly, how the hell was I going to get out of this mess in one piece when I'm stuck in the middle and being pulled in two different directions?

"Stuck In the Middle With You" – Stealers Wheel, 1972.

Except these weren't clown and jokers to my left and right; these people were dead serious and this was no laughing matter. We were now at the part of the circus where the high wire act was being performed without a net...and my acrobatic balancing act is starting to wobble big time.

Chapter 31

Brooklyn
2007

"Summer in the City" – Lovin' Spoonful, 1966.

Hot town, all right; the temperature was already unbearable and the sun had only been up on this Friday morning for a short time. It was going to be an especially scorching day for Barry Stone, who still found himself in the midst of the most frustrating few days of his life. The finest treasure in the collecting world had walked into his door, and now he was struggling to practically *give* it away.

He had agreed to lower his seller's commission to ten percent on this deal, so every extra million would net him another hundred thousand. He'd planned on making about two million on the transaction, and now he'd be lucky to get a quarter of that.

The bank had to have their money wired to them by five o'clock this afternoon or the whole reason for selling the sheet of cards was lost. Ludwig Braun's seven million dollar offer was enough to save the park, but Joe was adamant about not selling the cards to Braun. That left Jerry Johns' offer of five million as the highest, since those clowns at Duke had shocked him by pulling out of the race altogether. But why?

The only thing Stone could figure was that maybe Braun had made arrangements to turn around and sell the cards to Duke as soon as he bought them. That would be just like him to use his muscle and influence to get the sheet for seven million and then sell it for twelve or so to Duke. He'd make a quick five million dollar profit, and Duke would come out ahead since they would get the uncut sheet for twelve million instead of the twenty million they would have had to pay.

Stone's cell phone rang. He was still hiding out at his sister's place to keep from being found, so the call had to be from one of the few people who had this number. "Hello?" he said, flipping open his phone.

"Good morning, Mr. Stone," said Ludwig Braun in his recognizable voice. "I understand things seem to be breaking my way now that other buyers are waffling."

"I'm sure you had something to do with that, Mr. Braun," Stone said icily.

"Oh, Mr. Stone, I'm afraid the rumors of my nefarious activities are greatly exaggerated. You give me far more credit than I deserve," Braun stated coldly. "After all, I could have just had you kidnapped and tortured until you produced the sheet *if* I were truly that kind of evil man. Instead, I am willing to pay seven million dollars for it. How can anyone consider it a crime to pay so much money for something that has only intrinsic value?"

"What would be criminal," Stone said, "would be me selling the item for such a low price. But fortunately that won't happen, Mr. Braun, because Dr. Marinolli has specifically instructed me *not* to sell the item to you."

"*What?*" Braun exploded. "That's ridiculous! Why would he do that unless you gave him some cockamamie story about me blowing up your store?"

"The reason," Stone said, "is because you're German, and his father was killed by Germans in World War One."

"Oh that's rich," Braun sneered. "Did Dr. *Marinolli* forget what side the *Italians* were on in World War Two? Did he renounce his ancestry at that time and change his name to *Martin*?"

"Don't get mad at me, Mr. Braun, I'm just the messenger. If it makes you feel any better, I drive a BMW and love Beck's beer," Stone said seriously. "But I'm not the one calling the shots here."

"I see that," Braun said pensively. "Well, I'm sure some stroke of fortune will come my way today, so I will be calling you back later this afternoon to get the wiring instructions. Take care."

"The Heat is On" – Glenn Fry, 1984.

Chapter 32

Long Island
2007

"Scheisse!" Ludwig Braun yelled in German as he slammed his cell phone shut and threw it across the expansive library in his summer home. It exploded into pieces as it smashed into a marble bust of Beethoven. "Karl, get in here *now*!

"Yes, Mr. Braun, what do you need?" Karl huffed as he hurried into the room and stood at attention in front of Braun's desk. If Rocky Balboa had fought a German instead of a Russian, Karl would have gotten the role. He was as wide as he was tall, with a tight crew cut and massive torso.

"I need you to get Franz and do a job for me," Braun said with a look on his face of pure hatred. "It is one that our ancestors started almost a hundred years ago, and one that I will finish today. We're going to kill an Italian who doesn't like our ethnicity. His father was too weak to defeat our people, and now he will meet the same fate."

"What family is this one in?" Karl asked, assuming that this was just another mob-on-mob hit.

"Ha," Braun snickered, "this one is eighty-nine years old and bedridden alone in a Brooklyn hospital. I need it to look like an unsuspicious natural death – we're not sending a message to anyone here – so just smother him with the pillow. You should be able to get in and out of there in less than thirty seconds. Have Franz stand guard outside the room and it should be a snap."

"Yes sir, Mr. Braun!"

Braun continued giving orders to his henchman. "You go get Franz and make a run to the nearest medical supply shop to buy both of you some hospital scrubs and surgical masks. Then hurry back by here and I will have a letter to give you. It is absolutely imperative that this letter be left on the bedside table after you kill him. This letter must be found right away by anyone who comes in the room."

"Yes sir, Mr. Braun, you can count on me," Karl replied, hurrying off.

After Karl left, Braun went on-line to find what he was looking for. Within a matter of minutes, he had printed off a piece of stationary paper using the logo and address of the New York Methodist Hospital in Brooklyn. It took him a little while longer for his next item, but within fifteen minutes he was able to find what he needed: an example of Dr. Joe Marinolli's signature on a certificate of authenticity for a rare book that had sold at auction several years ago.

Braun printed out his letter on the counterfeit stationary using generic block letters in a shaky hand that nobody could ever prove were *not* the product of an eighty-nine year old man on his last leg. If the plan went off without a hitch, nobody would suspect a thing and nobody with any extensive training in handwriting would ever be called in to examine the letter anyway.

After he had practiced several times, Braun signed Dr. Marinolli's name to the bottom of the letter and read it back to himself one last time:

DEAR MR. STONE:

I DID NOT SLEEP WELL LAST NIGHT,
PERHAPS BECAUSE OF THE GUILT I FEEL IN
HARBORING BAD FEELINGS TOWARD A
MAN I HAVE NEVER MET, LUDWIG BRAUN.
I AM WRITING THIS FOR YOU IN CASE I
SHOULD BECOME UNABLE TO
COMMUNICATE OR, GOD FORBID, DIE.
I HAVE DECIDED THAT I DO WANT TO
SELL THE UNCUT WAGNER SHEET TO MR.
BRAUN IF HE IS THE HIGHEST BIDDER.
IT'S THE RIGHT THING TO DO, AS WE
SHOULD ALL TRY TO FORGET THE PAST.

YOURS TRULY,
Dr. Joseph Marinolli, Jr.

Chapter 33

Atlanta
2007

"It's Five O'clock Somewhere" – Jimmy Buffett, 2003.

I hear what Jimmy's saying, but it sure feels like five o'clock on this Friday's never going to arrive. I haven't left our office in more than two days, telling those who have asked that my apartment is being repainted and is therefore inaccessible. Of course, this draws clever retorts from everyone about how Kristi must be making me paint the apartment in pastel colors, so I have to save face and come up with a proper Malenglish response.

"Orange and blue -- Florida Gator colors everywhere," I lie with a straight face. "*Nobody* tells me what to do in *my* house!"

I'm the only one who catches the irony in this statement, since I'm actually being told *exactly* what to do by two different people right now: Jerry Johns and Kristi's kidnapper. Heck, make that *three* different people if you count Kristi, since her voice is the one that I keep hearing in my head, begging me to come through for her.

So here I am, camping out like Canteen Boy. The firm messenger has gone out on food runs for all of my meals, and I've even become so paranoid that I've shut my blinds. Yesterday I heard the window washers outside and thought for sure a paramilitary SWAT team was about to come crashing through. I was as paranoid as a kid sneaking peeks at his father's hidden issue of *Playboy*.

I looked at the clock again. Damn, had it gone *backwards*? This was like waiting for the final bell on the last day of the school year. It was still only 1:37 pm.

There has to be something I can do!

When exactly will I even know whether or not she's been released? What if the Wagner cards sell and I *still* don't hear from her or the kidnappers? How long am I supposed to wait before going to the Feds?

If I go too soon, the kidnappers may have already released Kristi, in which case me ratting them out is only going to put both of us in more danger than ever. But if I wait too long, the Feds will rake me over the coals and maybe lose precious time that they need to try and find her.

Or God help me, her body.

I clicked open the iTunes window on my computer and started playing "our song" again over the built-in speaker. I had been playing it over and over for good luck; it seemed to be the only thing that reassured me. It was a true Malenglish love song, one that Romeo probably sang about Juliet and Sir Lancelot about Guinevere.

I sang along softly, realizing that no truer lyrics had even been uttered. There I was, enjoying my pleasant memories of Kristi and weeping at the same time for fear of losing her. She was indeed bringing a smile to my face and a tear to my eye, my sweet Cherry Pie.

"She's My Cherry Pie" – Warrant, 1990.

Chapter 34

Brooklyn
2007

Joe Marinolli was watching CNN Headline News on the television in his hospital room, waiting to hear back from Barry Stone about the progress of the big sale. Joe knew that he was only a few hours away from the deadline to save Stratton Park, and he hoped that Barry Stone would deliver everything that he'd promised.

Joe wondered why the new orderly out in the hall was looking in at him with more interest than before. Joe didn't recognize this new guy, and didn't think he looked like a very compassionate caregiver.

The guy looked more like a drill sergeant, Joe thought to himself, hoping that *this* guy wouldn't be the one to insert his next catheter. He didn't even look like he believed in pain, much less in painkillers, Joe laughed to himself, turning down the volume and laying his head back for a short nap.

I guess being old has its virtues -- like being able to fall asleep at will -- Joe chuckled in his head as he faded to black. In seconds he was out like a light.

The next memory Joe recalled was dreaming about being trapped underwater, unable to breathe. Joe opened his eyes but was still in total darkness. He couldn't get any air; someone was suffocating him with a pillow!

Joe faded to black again, but this time it was much different. This time there was a bright light at the end of a tunnel and Joe's father was waiting for him, dressed in his Army uniform and still only twenty-three years old -- just as Joey had always seen him in pictures.

The last thought Joey had, as a melody started drifting though his thoughts, was, "Boy, do we have a lot to talk about, Dad."

"Cat's In the Cradle" – Harry Chapin, 1974.

Chapter 35

Somewhere near Savannah
2007

Kristi was really beginning to panic about her likelihood of surviving this ordeal. Her captors had told her initially that she would be released as soon as Chuck did whatever it was they wanted him to do. Then how come she was still here?

To her, it seemed as if a week or more had passed since she was abducted, as she had completely lost all sense of time. The realization that she was not the only kidnapping victim here at the warehouse gave her some comfort and hope for being rescued, but it also made her realize that these guys were pros and that she was not their first rodeo.

As Kristi sat on the couch watching -- well listening to, actually -- *Saturday Night Live's Best of Chris Farley* DVD, she made small talk with "Gale," the captor who had been in the back of the van with her. It was her way of staying sane and not losing her marbles. She tried to convince herself that they couldn't kill her if they liked her; it was all she could think of.

"How do you guys plan to let me go?" she asked.

"We don't plan anything. We just follow orders," he stated matter-of-factly.

"Well you guys wouldn't split and just leave me here by myself, would you?"

"We would if that's what we were told to do," he replied. "But Mr. Braun told us to be real careful because he doesn't want the heat from any murder rap, so I'm guessing that he would place an anonymous call to the authorities after we left to let them know where they could find you."

"Well that's a relief!" she said with a hint of sarcasm, keeping to herself the fact that she had just learned the name of the kidnapping ringleader.

"Aw, damn it! Look what you did, missy!" Gale bellowed a few seconds later. "You opened your trap and got me to talking, and now I've screwed up big time and told you the name of my boss. Jeez, I know he's not going to like that one damn bit!"

"Oh, no," Kristi pleaded, "I swear I'll never tell anyone what you said. Honest!"

"Oh, Lord," Gale said in genuine panic. "I don't think I can tell him, 'cause he'll just have me killed for being a loose talker. What the hell am I going to do about this?"

"Nothing!" Kristi shouted, knowing that she was dead meat for sure if the man behind this whole incident ever learned that she could finger him. "Don't tell anyone. I *swear* I'll never tell!"

"Tell what?" said another voice that had just entered the room unbeknownst to Kristi. It was not the voice of the van driver, who was normally friendly. This guy sounded dead serious.

"Oh, jeez, Jake, I screwed up big time! I slipped up and mentioned Braun's name in front of her," Gale cried out.

"You stupid ass, you just mentioned *my* name too!" the stranger screamed at him. "Now we may have no choice but to kill the girls and get ourselves out of here. We can just tell Braun that they tried to mutiny and we had no choice but to whack them."

Kristi heard the words and could feel herself spinning out of control. Her life was a hair away from being over.

"No, please no, Gale!" pleaded Kristi. "Please go out there and try to talk him out of it! I swear I'll never tell anyone!"

"Man, I don't know," Gale said nervously. "She's right though, let's at least go out here and figure out how we're going to handle this."

The door slammed and Kristi was alone in the room. Until now, she had never tried to remove her duct tape blindfold since she was cooperating fully and had no reason to risk angering her guards, but now things were different. Now she may only have a minute left to live, and she needed to be able to see if there was any chance of fleeing.

She began clawing furiously at the tape, ripping out huge chunks of hair and scalp in the process. It hurt worse than anything she had ever felt, but just as she was about to get it off, her optimism was ripped away when she heard a blood-curdling scream from a female somewhere down the hall. It had to be the other girl that she had heard being brought in earlier!

The scream was immediately followed by two loud gunshots that cracked the air and echoed terrifically in the old metal warehouse! Then all was silent.

Kristi was now clawing like a cat sliding off a roof to get the duct tape off of her eyes. Obviously they had decided that shooting the girls was their only option, and if she was going to be shot, the shooter was going to have to do it while staring her right in the eyes.

Just as she ripped the last piece off of her face and tried to get her eyes adjusted to light again, she heard the door open behind her and she leaped up to face her executioner, fully prepared to fight to the death. Before she could even flinch, however, a man she didn't recognize came into the room with a huge pistol in his hand.

This had to be the new voice that Kristi had just heard, and she knew immediately that she had no chance. The guy was as solid as a bull and reminded her of Sergeant Hulka from *Stripes*. The stranger raised his gun and Kristi felt herself start to faint.

"Goodbye, Chuck," she thought, as elevator music started playing in her head:

"The Night the Lights Went Out in Georgia" – Vicki Lawrence, 1973.

Chapter 36

Atlanta
2007

"*Too Much Time On My Hands*" – Styx, 1981.

"Barry Stone on line three, Chuck," Angie buzzed. I looked at the clock, agonizing that it was still only 1:55 pm. Time was frozen in place.

"Hey, Barry," I said tiredly. "Anything new?"

"Unfortunately, a *lot* is new, and none of it good. Joe Marinolli died today before he could see his treasure come to fruition. At least he went peacefully in his sleep."

"Oh man, that's too bad," I said solemnly. "From everything you've told me, the guy had a heart as big as a redwood."

"No doubt about it," Barry agreed, "but unfortunately it was as old as one too. It finally just gave out."

Then it hit me, and I started to panic. "So you won't be able to sell the card now?" I asked, fearing that Kristi would now have to remain in custody for a much longer period of time. This was the *worst* news that I could have heard.

"No, this won't have any affect on the sale of the T-206 Wagner sheet," Barry said, giving me great relief. "I'm under contract to conduct the sale, so the sale will go on as planned. The only change is that the money will go to Dr. Marinolli's estate instead of him personally. Granted, his estate has all been bequeathed to the orphanage, so they'll still get the money, but it just may not be in time to save the orphanage."

"That stinks," I said, unable to come up with anything more eloquent or descriptive.

"No doubt," Barry agreed. "But Joe Marinolli did leave a note indicating that I was approved to sell the card to Ludwig Braun, the German buyer. Apparently Joe had a change of heart overnight. So that means Braun's offer of seven million is the current high bid. What do you say, Chuck, can I talk you into paying eight for it? You know it's worth a lot more than that, and I'm hoping you've just been holding back your best offer until the end. We're pretty much there now; Dr. Marinolli has certainly reached his end."

This was it. This was where I had to choose between disbarment and disgracing my family name versus trying to save the life of the girl I had fallen madly in love with. In my typical Malenglish fashion, I tried to think what various movie stars had done under these terms.

Robert Redford, as Roy Hobbs, had chosen his old sweetheart over a baseball career. John Belushi, as Jake

Blues, had chosen playing with his band over marrying his fiancée. Where did I fall on that spectrum? All-American boy or degenerate pig?

I heard myself tell Barry, "Sorry, Barry, but I just don't think we're in the market for it. I really wish I could help you. At least you have a buyer who can pay seven million for it. That's nothing to sneeze at, and hopefully you can use the sale documents to float a bridge loan to save the park."

I could hear the prison doors slamming shut in my head as I was hanging up the phone. I began to wonder what it would be like to be a fugitive living in a van down by the river with jack squat to my name.

No, I haven't done the research yet to see whether saving someone's life is a defense to legal malpractice in the State of Georgia, but right now I'd be happy with that outcome. It would at least mean that Kristi had survived.

Forty years I make it without falling in love and without getting into any trouble. The minute I let a woman into my heart, my life goes to hell in a hand basket.

Now I know how Romeo felt about Juliet -- and Sampson towards Delilah. But when they kissed?

"Fire" – The Pointer Sisters, 1979.

Chapter 37

Atlanta
2007

Four o'clock.

One hour to go until this freakin' mess is behind me.

I hope. Either that, or a much bigger mess begins.

Suddenly my mind started racing through one last scenario.

"What if Kristi is too good to be true because she *isn't* true?" I thought to myself. "What if I've been played like a fiddle by someone who just wanted to buy the card without Jerry Johns being in the mix? What if Kristi was a plant who was instructed to come on to me and then lure me into this trap?"

It all made sense to me now. This whole thing was a set up, and I had taken the bait; hook, line and sinker. There was no kidnapping. Kristi was in with whoever it was that bought off Alex, and all of them were conspiring to keep me from buying that card.

What an idiot I had been! I felt dumber than Cousin Eddie, and I didn't have a metal plate in my head that I could blame it on.

"What now?" I wondered. Do I call Barry and start bidding on the card? Do I call the Georgia Bar and report Alex? Or do I call the cops and report all of them for extortion?

I opened my desk drawer to pull out my phone book, and as I was reaching in to grab it, made a mental note to myself that my pistol was in there as well. I have a concealed weapons permit, but rarely carry the gun except when I have to walk to my car late at night. It was loaded, but a lot of good it was doing me now.

Or maybe it *was* going to come in handy, because the shit had just hit the fan. Alex, Kristi and Sergeant Hulka had all three just barged into my office without any warning and slammed the door shut! I guess I'd have been more surprised to see the Pope, Elvis and JFK...but not by much.

Hulka's eyes went immediately to the gun protruding from my drawer. "Freeze!" he yelled as he sprung into a crouch, whipping his huge automatic out of his shoulder holster and pointing it right at me.

Fortunately, I had instinctively drawn my gun and found myself pointing it right back at him; arms locked and knees bent ever so slightly. We were locked in a stare down that somebody was bound to lose, and I was determined that it wouldn't be me.

If I was going to be sued for malpractice posthumously, at least I was going to give my defense attorney another dead body to blame it on. The only question going through my head was which of the other two I would shoot first after killing the gunman. They had both betrayed me to the core.

Chapter 38

Atlanta
2007

Nobody moved a muscle, and you could actually smell the aroma of perspiration emanating from everyone involved. A bead of sweat dripped down my forehead and into my eye, but I couldn't wipe it without exposing myself for an instant. Maybe if I had paid more attention in law school I would have remembered what to do in this situation.

"Please drop your weapon, Mr. Evans!" the man with a crew cut finally managed to yell. "I'm F.B.I.!"

"Yeah," I replied, holding my pistol aimed steadily at his torso, "and I'm with the frickin' mattress police. Sorry, Hulka, but I ain't buying it."

"He's serious, Chuck, really!" Kristi exclaimed to my right, but I couldn't turn that way for fear of losing eye contact with my opponent.

"Sorry," I said firmly, "but I'm wise to all three of you now. I was such a sucker for your game, but now there's no way you can all get out of here without getting caught unless you killed everyone in the office on your way up," I said.

About that time, I realized that the three of them had made it all the way into my office without anyone having buzzed me that they were coming. Shit! Maybe they *had* killed all the others in the office!

The silence was deafening, until mercifully it was broken by Angie buzzing through on the intercom in her normal bored tone. "Chuck, it's Barry Stone on line four," she said. "He wants to know if you've talked with the F.B.I. yet. I told him you were in with them right now."

I looked at Hulka again, and he nodded his head slowly to show that he was under control and that I was on the verge of making a big mistake.

"Mr. Evans," he said, "my identification is in my inside jacket pocket. I'm going to put my gun down slowly now and then open my jacket very slowly so that you can watch me reach into my pocket with two fingers to pull it out. Please don't shoot me in the meantime."

He did as he said he would, and I watched with wonder as he pulled out a badge and identification card that proved he was indeed Federal Agent Oliver Anderson.

"So what the hell is going on?" I asked in a stupor. Then I turned to Kristi. "Oh crap! You really *were* kidnapped?"

She nodded.

"Oh my God, I'm so glad you made it!" I screamed. "I was worried sick!"

Kristi and I lunged towards each other and embraced in a huge hug. I was afraid to let her go, and I think I may have broken one or two of her ribs in my excitement.

"So what happened? Who took you? Where'd you go? How did you escape?" I had more questions than a freshman midterm.

Angie buzzed in again, oblivious to what was going on inside my office. "Chuck, do you want to talk to Barry Stone?"

"No," I said, "tell him too busy to talk and I'll be back in touch later. Frankly, I could care less about his baseball card right now."

I turned suddenly to Alex and asked, "How did you fit into all of this? Did you get my e-mails?"

"You'll have to get details from Kristi about where she was and what she went through. But from what I've heard, they actually treated her pretty good, right Kristi?"

Kristi nodded, still holding me tight and crying into my shoulder. "I'm fine, I'm fine," she murmured into my chest. "Thank you Chuck for following the kidnappers' instructions and saving my life."

I stroked the back of her head and squeezed her tight.

Alex continued. "Chuck, here's what I can tell you on my end. That night I disappeared, the people from Duke had called me back that afternoon and made one final pitch to get me on their side. They offered me a job as assistant general counsel for the university at $450,000 a year, but they also offered me the exclusive right to be the player agent representative for all of their basketball players who would go pro in the future. Can you imagine, being the agent for every Duke player in the NBA? That would be incredible!"

Chuck nodded in agreement, realizing that Duke's offer was so good that he couldn't really blame Alex for taking it.

"But I wasn't going to take it, Chuck. I was going to call them back in the morning and tell them to pound sand. This firm has been good to me when I needed it, and I'd rather earn my way to the top than have it handed to me as part of some underhanded plot."

Chuck looked at Alex with amazement.

"But then that night, I got a visit at home from good old Agent Anderson here and some of his friends. That scared the crap out of me, that's for sure. I didn't know *what* was going on.

As it turns out, the Duke Foundation had already been in contact with the F.B.I. because the fifteen-year-old daughter of the Foundation Chairman had been kidnapped that afternoon just after they had called me. Apparently the people at Duke reacted differently than you did, Chuck. They called the F.B.I. immediately and filled them in on the entire Honus Wagner baseball card saga."

Chuck looked sheepishly at Agent Anderson and grimaced. "I know I should have called you too, but I hope you can understand why I couldn't. I didn't want to have her blood on my hands."

"I understand," Agent Anderson said, "but it sure would have made our job a lot easier."

"Heck, I saw you following me that day at Kristi's work and then at my apartment, so I was convinced you were in with the kidnappers," I told him.

"That's okay, Chuck, since they were convinced that *you* were in with the kidnappers!" Alex said laughing. "That's why Agent Anderson showed up at my house with his men. They grilled me left and right that night, and I assured them that you were *not* involved in the plot to kidnap the chairman's daughter just so that your client could win the Wagner sheet.

I'm not sure they believed me, so they told me to just gather up all my stuff and clear out for a while until they could sort through everything. Sorry if I scared you, but I wasn't going to cross the F.B.I."

"You thought *I* was a suspect?" I asked Anderson in amazement?

"Everyone was a suspect at that point. Then, when your girlfriend also showed up missing the next day, we started to think you might be in the clear. But then again, you could have just killed her off to make it *look* like she too had been kidnapped. We couldn't take any chances," Anderson stated.

"You know what really cleared you as a suspect, Chuck?" Alex asked. "Your e-mails to me! You clearly believed that I was in with the kidnappers, and your messages made it clear that you were not. Had you been in with them, there is no way you would have sent messages to me essentially confessing your involvement or bringing me into the mess when you had no idea where I even was."

"So you *did* get them?"

"Yep, and I made sure Agent Anderson saw them as soon as they came in. I felt like I was arguing before the Supreme Court trying to convince the Feds that you were in the clear!"

"Okay, so once you stopped thinking I was a criminal, how did you ever figure out who was *really* behind everything?" I wondered out loud.

Agent Anderson took over from here. "Earlier today, our Brooklyn branch office got a call from the New York City Police Department. It turns out that they had assigned some undercover officers to guard Dr. Marinolli in his hospital room at the insistence of Barry Stone.

Mr. Stone was suspicious that someone might try to harm Mr. Marinolli, and was persuasive enough to get someone's attention. Sure enough, they arrested two known felons dressed in scrubs, one of whom tried to smother Dr. Marinolli with a pillow."

"Wait a minute," I interrupted. "You said *tried* to smother Dr. Marinolli. Are you telling me that he *isn't* dead? Barry Stone told me earlier that he had passed away in his sleep!"

"Yes, that's what I'm telling you. Dr. Marinolli is alive and well. Mr. Stone was simply following his orders to get the word out that these criminals had succeeded in their task. We needed their boss to think his plan had worked, and we couldn't afford to have *anyone* know otherwise."

"I'll be damned," I said, shaking my head to try and keep everything clear. "All right, so then what?"

"At this point, we knew from Stone who it was that was trying to buy his card, and we knew from the Duke folks that the kidnapper was going to be trying to buy the card. It was just a matter of squeezing the two thugs from the hospital hard enough and confronting them with everything we knew.

Sure enough, they rolled over on Braun and told us everything, including who the leak was from Duke to Braun and where Braun's men had taken Kristi and Meagan. That's the name of the chairman's daughter. We got a crew assembled in Savannah as quickly as possible, and I got over there in time to lead the charge into the warehouse to free the girls."

"Don't feel bad, sweetheart," Kristi said to me with a smile, "Sergeant Hulka was the first thought I had too when I saw Agent Anderson at the warehouse. I thought for sure he was going to kill me, just like you did!"

"So have you arrested Braun yet?" I asked.

"Not yet, they can't locate him. But I can assure you that he can't hide forever. I'm sure he'll hire a stable of lawyers – pardon the pun – and deny any involvement whatsoever. Who knows whether it will work or not?

But either way, he's out seven million dollars, because we had Barry Stone call him and give him wiring instructions for the money to buy the card. Stone told him that he had won and that the sheet would be his today at five o'clock, delivered wherever Braun wanted it delivered.

This was *before* Braun got word that his hired kidnappers had been killed and his hostages had been freed. He thought he had pulled it off, so the money was wired and is not custody of the United States Government."

"That's awesome!" I howled in laughter, starting to finally realize that everything was going to turn out fine in the end.

But wait!

What had I done?

I scrambled to my door and flung it open.

"Angie! Get Barry Stone back on the phone. Hurry!"

Chapter 39

Brooklyn
2007

"I was wondering if I was going to hear back from you," Barry said half-jokingly. "I'm sitting here at the hospital on speakerphone with Dr. Marinolli and Tom Bennett from the orphanage. Chuck, you've never met Joe Marinolli, but it's about time your paths finally cross."

"Hello, Chuck," Joe said, and like that I had finally come in direct contact with the historical lineage behind the rarest and more incredible memorabilia item in collecting history. I felt something pass through me like the spirits of past Marinollis; Joe's father, his mother, and his father's father. They were all an integral part of this incredible journey.

"Hello, Joe," I said. "I haven't spoken to a dead man since we used the Ouija board back in sixth grade. It's amazing what they can do with fiber optics these days."

Everyone laughed.

"Sorry about that, Chuck," Barry chimed in. I knew you weren't a part of the plot, but I didn't know who you were in contact with down there. The F.B.I. couldn't risk any leaks, so I hope you understand."

"Yeah, I do. And I hope you understand why I could never tell you about Kristi being kidnapped and everything. I was afraid it would get her killed."

"Perfectly understandable, Chuck," Joe said. "I'm just thankful that Barry had a premonition after telling Braun that I was refusing to sell him the card. Barry's instincts told him that Braun would try something dirty, and thankfully he did or we may never have solved this mess in time."

"Well, that's precisely what I want to talk to you about," I said, looking at the clock and seeing that it was 4:13.

"With Braun out of the bidding, is our five million dollar offer still the high bid?" I asked.

"No, I'm afraid that once Braun was discovered and the Duke chairman's daughter was safe, they entered back into the fray. They're going to buy the uncut sheet for ten million."

"Like hell they are!" I shouted into the speakerphone, Kristi and Alex huddled over my shoulder. "This thing ain't over! We'll pay you eleven million."

Everyone in the hospital room cheered in delight.

"Atta boy, Chuck!" Barry said. "I knew you would come through once Braun was off your back. Let me conference in the representative from Duke and we can all discuss this together.

"Please just hurry, Barry" Tom Bennett said eagerly, "because we still have to get the money wired to the bank before five in order to keep Stratton Park."

"Get them on the phone, Barry," I said loudly in my excitement. "It's time to make that orphanage some money, because the price of poker just went up! If those Duke boys want to get this sheet of cards, you let 'em know that they're up against Boss Hogg!"

"Just the Good Ol' Boys" – Waylon Jennings, 1979.

Chapter 40

Atlanta
2007

By now, the atmosphere in our room was electric. We had the emotions of Kristi and Alex coming back into the fold, plus the tension of being involved in a fierce bidding war that was really starting to heat up. Jim had now joined us in my office, although it took all of us to keep him from attacking Alex at first sight. After hearing the whole story, Jim and Alex were back together again, like black and white negative images of each other that had never been apart.

Barry had called us back once he had patched Richard Wigginton into the call. It was Wigginton who was speaking now.

"Mr. Stone, I understand that a bid has been placed at eleven million dollars, is that correct?"

"Yes, and now the bidding is back to you," Barry replied. "Will you go to twelve?"

"Yes, we will."

I had my finger on the mute button on our end until it was my turn to talk, allowing all of us to confer without being heard.

"Dang it," Jim said. "They've got more money than most small countries. How are we going to outbid them?"

"Hold on a sec," I said as I released the mute button.

"We will go to fifteen million, Barry."

I pushed the button back down and turned to Jim. "I want them to see how serious we are. They're the ones who *have* to have these cards in order to avoid potential litigation. Let's see if we can't get them to understand what they're in for."

I turned to Alex. "Go tell Angie to get Jerry Johns on his cell phone ASAP. Tell her to keep calling and to call the team clubhouse number if she can't get him on his cell."

Wigginton coughed. "Mr. Stone, the Duke Foundation is prepared to pay *twenty* million for the sheet."

There was a stunned silence in our room, while Joe and Tom could be heard celebrating loudly in Brooklyn.

"If Mr. Evans' client is willing to top that offer," Wigginton said seriously, "he runs a very big risk of having to put his money where his mouth is and could potentially end up paying twenty-one million dollars for a sheet of cardboard that may not be the only one in existence. Who knows what may come out of the woodwork tomorrow?"

Just then, Alex came into the room with his cell phone out, indicating that Jerry "Big Stick" Johns was on the line. I excused myself momentarily from the conference call and let them know that I would be right back.

I stepped outside in the hall and had a heart-to-heart conversation with the Stickman, letting him know some ideas that had come to me. We were on the same page when we hung up, and I had a good feeling about how this thing was going to turn out.

"This is Chuck," I said into the phone. "I'm back on the line now, and my client is indeed willing to pay twenty-one million. He sees this as a competition now, and he isn't accustomed to losing."

Everyone in the room looked at me as if I had just swallowed a sword; their mouths agape and their eyes as big as pool balls. I held up a palm as if to show them that I knew what I was doing, but only I knew that the next move on Duke's part would make or break my future.

"Twenty-two million," Wigginton finally said after a long pause, realizing that his bluff had been called and he was stuck in the pot for the duration now. My ploy had worked.

Again, the jubilance in that Brooklyn hospital room could be heard in Atlanta, probably even if we hadn't been on the phone. They were beside themselves up there, and for good reason.

"Twenty-five million," I snapped as soon as Wigginton had finished. "And this could go all night." Again, I had to hold my hand to make sure nobody in our room blurted out something that might destroy our leverage.

A gasp could be heard on the other end of the line.

"But I might remind you," I continued, "that Mr. Johns has always had sort of a complex about skipping college and going straight from high school into professional baseball. I know it would mean the world to him if he could be awarded an honorary degree from a school as prestigious as Duke."

"That could certainly be arranged," Wigginton said after a short pause, picking up on where this might be headed.

"And I also think the proposal that was given to my associate Alex is a fair one; that every future Duke basketball player hire our firm to represent them upon entering the NBA. These accounts will be split evenly between Alex and Jim."

Wigginton got off the line to confer briefly with his cohorts, and then came back on. "That can also be arranged with no problem, Mr. Evans, if need be. Your firm's reputation is such that we would be happy to sign such a contract."

"And I suppose a four-year full ride scholarship for one Kristi Dickson would be an easy request to fulfill, considering what she went through to get us all here?"

Wigginton didn't hesitate on that one. "Consider it done. We would be honored."

I thought Kristi was going into convulsions over to my left, but apparently it was just some sort of victory dance. I would have to work with her on that; it was like the infamous Elaine Benes dance. Calling it "lame" would have been too kind.

"Then with those three conditions in place, our proposal is that Jerry Johns gets to buy the sheet for twenty-five million and then turns around and sells it to the Duke Foundation for thirty-five million. Otherwise, we just sit here and go back and forth forever."

Barry Stone jumped in at this point. "Chuck, can I talk to you for a second on another line?"

I called Barry on my cell phone.

"Chuck, what are your doing?" he asked incredulously.

"Well, one time, at band camp…," I started before he cut me off.

"Stop, Chuck, I'm being serious. What you are proposing is called "bid collusion" and I can't allow it since it will severely curtail the final selling price for my consignor's item."

"Barry, you need to pass *this* confidential information on to your clients, and then decide how you want to handle it from here. What you and your clients don't know is that when I spoke with Jerry Johns, he told me *not* to bid any higher than the twenty million that was on the table. Therefore, if you won't allow my proposal to take place, we will simply retract our last few offers and Duke will get the card for twenty million."

"But then it was shill bidding that I also can't allow," Stone said.

"Oh no, not at all," I assured him. "I absolutely want to buy the card for twenty-five million and keep it. I can talk Johns into coming up with the rest, even if the firm has to loan it to him for now in order to close the deal. We want the card, so we were not just shilling for your consignor.

But, we also realize that we can *never* outbid them, so why not let it end here, where *everyone* comes out ahead? Go talk to your clients and then let's see if Duke will even go for the plan anyway. They may just tell us to go pound sand."

"Plus," I continued, "this is not really a public auction in the true sense of the word, as it is not open to the general public and it has not been registered as such. This is just an informal sales discussion. None of the legal rules for auctions apply; I looked it up. Hell, you can't lose at this point Barry. There's no way the orphans are going to die poor and penniless, still trying to play a phonograph record with a peanut."

Barry chuckled before hanging up, and then rejoined the conference call a moment later. "After conferring with everyone on this end, we have decided that we would be perfectly satisfied with the plan that Mr. Evans has laid out.

Alternatively, we would of course be happy to see the bidding continue all night. Mr. Wigginton, the ball is in your court, sir."

"I was discussing it with my group while you were on the phone with Mr. Evans," Wigginton said proudly, "and we would be delighted to have the auction end now so that we can enter into a binding contract for sale from Mr. Johns to our foundation for thirty-five million."

I couldn't believe it; everything had worked out! Stratton Park was now safe in the hands of the orphanage forever, as they would have plenty of extra money from this sale to keep them from having to borrow against the land ever again; Jerry Johns had made a quick and easy ten million dollars for doing nothing; the firm had just picked up millions of dollars worth of revenue and publicity by getting the exclusive Duke basketball deal; and Kristi was going to Duke for free.

It was a quick and easy plane ride from Atlanta to Durham and back, so I knew that I would have no problem making the long distance relationship work. Then again, with the firm having the new Duke contract, we would need a full time person working in Durham anyway, and as Ulysses "Everett" McGill would say, "*I'm voting for yours truly!*"

"*Man of Constant Sorrow*" – The Soggy Bottom Boys, 2000.

Chapter 41

Botswana
2007

"Chuck, it's Dad. Can you hear me? We finally got back to civilization where I could grab a phone. Sorry I haven't called in earlier. How's everything going at work? Anything new? Everything under control?"

The senior Mr. Evans leaned into the phone booth to escape the hot wind that was blowing sand into his face.

"What's that? I can barely hear you." He covered his other ear with his palm and tried his best to ascertain what was being said. He finally smiled.

"Good, I'm glad nothing happened out of the ordinary. I'm always scared that all Hell will break lose when I'm gone. Glad to hear it was just business as usual. I love you, kiddo, and I'll see you in a few days."

He turned to his friend who had accompanied him on the trip as they walked back to the jeep.

"Everything's fine, which is a good thing. I'm just not sure Chuck's ready to really handle things under pressure on his own yet."

Final Note

Dear Reader:

If you enjoyed this novel in the least, *please* do me the favor of recommending it to as many people as you know who you think will appreciate the humor and the intrigue. Being that this is my first novel, I had to pay out of my own pocket to publish it. Thus, while I'm begging you to please pass the copy you are holding in your hands around to as many people as possible…I'm not too proud to ask you to please buy as many copies as you like for gifts to others.

"Ain't Too Proud to Beg" – The Temptations, 1966.

The easiest and quickest way to order copies is on-line at any of these locations:

www.LuLu.com
www.Amazon.com
www.BooksAMillion.com

From there, you can easily find the book by typing the title or even just some buzz words in the "search" box at the top of the page.

Thanks for your time, and hopefully you'll stop by and let me know your thoughts at my blog:

www.Malenglish.com

- Hal

LaVergne, TN USA
19 December 2009
167539LV00006B/21/A